# ALEXANDRAYA

# PRUDENCE WILLETT

# ALEXANDRAYA

## DIVINE DESTINIES BOOK 2

A catalogue record for this book is available from the
National Library of Australia.
ISBN:  978-0-6456992-4-1 (ebook)
ISBN:  978-0-6456992-5-8 (paperback)

Cover designed by MiblArt
Map created by Lawson Willett
Chapter art designed by Abigail Jane Wilkins

For those of you who love. And love to hate.

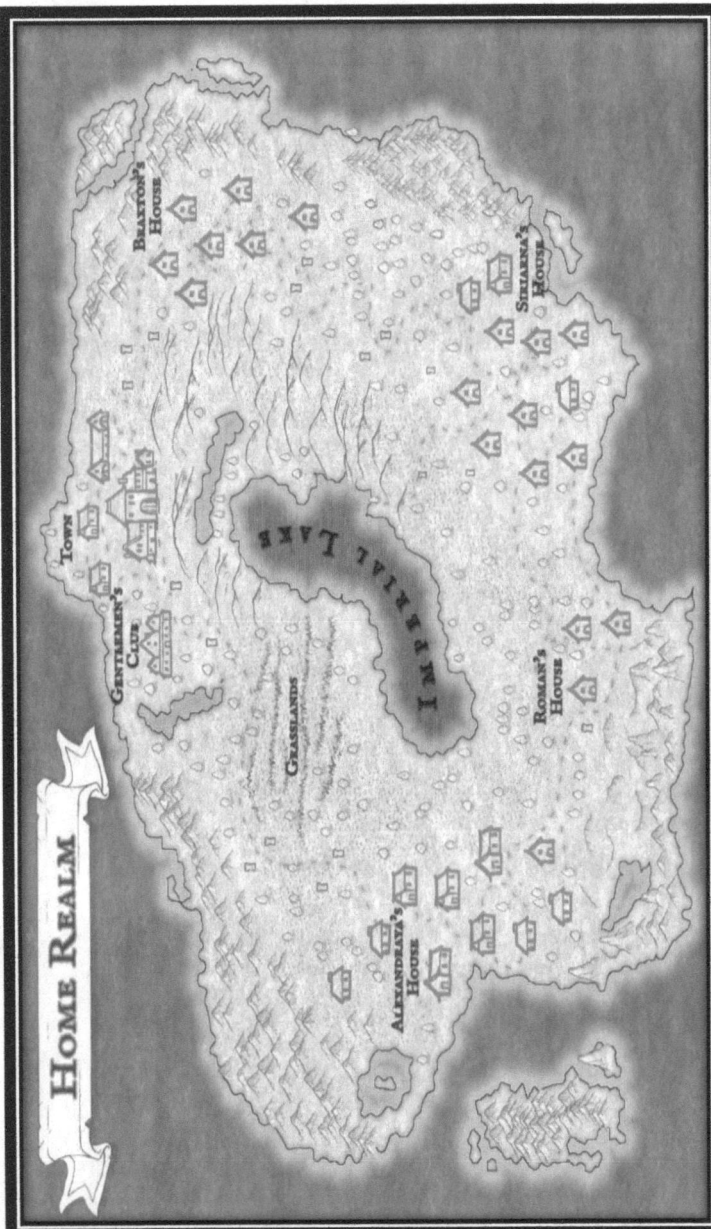

HOME REALM

# CHAPTER 1

## Alexandraya

My breathing is incessantly rapid. My heart is beating precipitously beneath my flesh. And my ears are deafened by vicious thoughts. I should be toasting nectar with my fellow immortals. But here I am, sitting practically alone in the sumptuous living room of Hermes' palace. It should be mine. Ours. My body convulses into involuntary shudders at the sight of my still yellow Propensity finger. Black smoke engulfs my soul, and my eyes sting, tarnished with hatred.

*Damn you to the Furies, Siriarna.*

A shrill whistle echoes around the enormous space as I tear strips from the wedding dress that clings to my body like a sordid rag. My nails continue to claw at the material until I am left naked, vertical in a pool of silk.

"All will be as it should," Psyche says rushing forward, wrapping her robes around my rigid frame.

I try to find comfort in her gesture, but all I see is the seduction of red dancing before my eyes. And I *want* to embrace it. Looking down at the once beautiful wedding dress destroyed by the herculean storm wielded by Siriarna, I plead a silent vow... *Make her pay.*

"I don't know what I would have done if you weren't at the ceremony, Psyche. And thank you for being here with me now." I say with real-feeling gratitude.

"Ahem," interrupts my fiancé.

"And you too, of course, Hermes," I say, my mouth twisting into a hollow smile.

"My love, please don't despair. I will have this whole situation remedied in no time, and we will be bound. Just as I promised," he says, thrusting Psyche aside.

Stepping closer, I rest my head against his toned, lean torso, and let out a deep sigh. "I believe in you," I whisper staring up at his ravenous gaze.

Psyche notices it too. "I think I'll leave you two to it," she says retreating toward the palace entry doors.

Her wings are barely at a flutter, and her pace is

abnormally sluggish. The strain creasing her normally flawless, angelic face is a reflection of today's shocking revelations about her past indiscretion with the King of Gods.

"Please come back any time, Psyche. Our door is always open," I say wholeheartedly.

There is a slight edge to my voice as actuality stabs my conscious—Psyche is Siriarna's biological mother, and I wish she was mine. Is blood thicker than water? By rights, we are related, my ancestry lies with her sister—an ancient and long deceased mortal. Disgust at Siriarna's luck in having a great goddess as her mother while my own was mortally fragile makes my stomach churn.

"Time for some rest," Hermes says abruptly, scooping me into his arms with ease. His strength is seduction overload to my senses.

My body is abnormally stiff, and I know exactly what I need for unwinding the knotty tension clutching its core. After all, my solace is rough play and this is what lured Hermes into an eternal partnership.

Images of Julienne rush to my mind as do the trials she set during my youth. They started out straightforward, like withstanding moments in a darkened room, or holding my breath for elongated periods of time under the serene waters of the Imperial Lake in the Home Realm.

The trials she set were to prepare me for life as an elite semi god. One who should eventually capture the attention of a god—that was the ultimate goal. The only goal. Gradually these trials increased in severity. I used to scream when the wooden batten pounded my flesh. But as the years advanced, when I returned to the Home Realm at the end of Evolirium's semesters, I found my guide mother's beatings more a caress, a welcomed comfort. A release for my tension. I need that release now. "Let's go," I answer huskily.

******

Exhaling a deep satisfied breath, I gaze at the sleeping god next to me. He is magnificent in every sense of the word and his prowess in the bedroom has left my body tingling. Watching the way his chest rises and falls in perfect harmony is hypnotising in its rhythm, and I find myself unable to drag my eyes away.

When I untangle my body from Hermes' clench and slide out of bed, my feet slap the marble floor brutally as I tumble from its height. And I curse out loud at my stature inadequacy. Hermes does not stir.

Red flashes before my eyes and I falter, dizzy from the vision. Clinging to the bed frame above me, I inhale a deep breath and squeeze my eyes shut until the image vanishes. Then I grab the chiton crumpled at my feet, and creep from the room—even though I'm sure a thunder of horses would not disturb my lover.

Down the staircase I trail, and through the palace I roam until I arrive at the conservatory. My favourite room in the palace. I love the way it's surrounded by windows, capturing my reflection from every angle, and this morning is no different. In the glass, a mirrored smile stares back at me, and I twirl. I spin faster and faster, my hair a rambling cascade of silk shadowing my movements, and I stretch out my arms dropping the chiton as I pirouette. Spent of breath, I collapse into the enormous couch that swallows my body whole.

"Alexandraya?" Hermes' smooth velvet-like voice sails into the room.

"I'm here," I say through ragged breaths.

In two steps, Hermes is above me, dropping a kiss on my forehead. "Yes, I *see* you," he says hotly.

Laughing, I wriggle from the couch, scoop up the simple white chiton, and drape the fabric around my body, fastening it at the shoulder. The excess material piles at my feet, and I reach down to tear the length. But Hermes beats me to it, "I think I'll make the adjustments this time," he winks, gently removing my hands from the fabric. "Although, I'd be happy for you to remain naked at all times within these palace walls."

"Your wish is my command," I say, caressing the fabric.

Hermes traces his fingers from my ankle to my calf. His touch is delicate, like a fluttering of eyelashes over my skin. And my pulse begins to race. In a split second, the material tears as he expertly pulls at the fabric until it sits evenly above my knee. It's the most seductive sound I've ever heard. "There you go," he says.

I lower my head to conceal the rosiness staining my cheeks. "Not bad Your Great."

"Perfect, as you are. Now, my love, I have a meeting with Zeus. I will sort out this ridiculous stall in proceedings and set a new date for our ceremony. I won't be long."

"I will think of nothing until your return." I reply

sweetly.

He lifts my chin with one hand, and strokes my cheek with the other, "If I was to bring you flowers for your patience, what colour would please you?"

Without a second thought, I say, "Red."

A fleeting kiss brushes my lips, and Hermes disappears in a speedy golden flash of light.

Now alone, I collapse back onto the couch, my mind free to explore the intrusive imagery haunting its corners. Closing my eyes, a sea of red fills my thoughts. Sifting through the tinge, a shape begins to form. Not a shape, a gather of silhouettes. But a persistent knocking distracts my concentration, and the image vanishes before I can identify its origin.

Marching to the entrance, I swing open the door with a tight-lipped smile. Which is immediately wiped away when I find Roman standing there, enveloped by the afternoon glow. "Hello, Alexandraya. Can we talk?" he asks.

"Okay, Roman," I say with a sigh, and step to the side.

I direct him to the front parlour and take a seat on one of the bulky carved chairs arranged in a semi-circle, my feet propped on the black velvet footstool at its base.

Roman sits beside me, one vacant chair between us.

Raking a hand through his immaculate sandy hair, he says, "What happened to *us*?"

*Gods, this is going to be awkward.*

"I'm not sure I understand the question," I say pouting.

His normally sanguine temperament is replaced with a savage sharpness. "Seriously?! I thought we were in love." he says through gritted teeth.

"We had a great time, Roman. But it wasn't love for me. Please understand, I didn't try to hurt you. That was never my intention. You're a great guy, and I wish the very best for you." I concentrate all my efforts on sounding sincere. It seems to be working because his shoulders slump, and his eyes no longer hold resentment.

"When did you hook up with Hermes?" he asks.

I knew it was coming, it's the question he came here to ask. I don't want any bad blood between us, but ultimately, he will be returning to Evolirium, and I will remain here in the Sky Realm... where I belong.

"I met him after the Third Quarter Challenge. We just clicked, Roman. I'm really very sorry," I say squeezing a tear from my right eye.

"It's okay. I guess you couldn't help it," he says.

Now that's the Roman I know, and could have possibly loved.

# CHAPTER 2

## Alexandraya

A burst of light flashes through the room signalling Hermes' return. He flies straight into the Conservatory, where I have just managed to settle myself after Roman's departure. The instant arrival and lack of warning is quite alarming. In fact, I find it a little creepy. The speed in which my husband-to-be is able to appear is something I'll need to be mindful of. I don't want him entering at any given moment catching me off guard. Although, I do love those golden winged sandals.

*Hmm, I wonder if they'll fit me in the future.*

"Great news my love, Zeus has agreed to reset our wedding... in one year."

"You've got to be kidding," I wail. I'm in utter shock.

A year! That's ridiculous.

"A year will sail by. Besides, we've got eternity. There's no rush. I thought Zeus was rather generous, considering his focus is elsewhere—"

His voice trails off as he realises his mistake. My teeth clench so tightly, my jaw aches at the strain. And when it loosens, I don't hold back the spell that seeps from my lips.

> "Light to me, come at force;
> Go now, hit your course."

An ear-piercing chime rings through the conservatory as a river of glass shatters, blanketing the floor beneath. My yellow Propensity finger remains pointed at the now empty barrier. The malicious release startles me, but the growing warmth filling my body is too much a comfort to guilt my action. A glint from a shard of glass catches my attention and on closer inspection, I see a hint of red reflected.

"Alexandraya—"

"I'm fine," I say brusquely. "I need time to myself." And I stalk from the room.

The palace door slams in my wake. I understand Hermes is not to blame for this whole wedding fiasco, but the fact that he's prepared to wait a year for our union infuriates me. I want to be a god. *Now*. My head is a cluster of thorny images, and the tension returns to my body, strangling my muscles like malevolent vines.

At least Hermes had the good sense not to follow me.

I have the urgent need to release more magic. Whilst not as powerful as I will become, my prior display in the conservatory gave me a burst of euphoria. Usually that energy occurs after a humanity mission, a kind of built-in semi god seduction implanted by the Fates. But the incident in the palace was a heady mix of dangerous ecstasy. An unsuspected seed imbedding itself in the darkest corner of my mind.

Using my Light Propensity, I speed around the Sky Realm searching for a place of solace. Beads of sweat form across my brow as I continue to scour the realm—my instincts propelling me to discover sanctum.

But as time glides past, I'm stuck zooming listlessly through the realm. About to abandon hope of finding the reprieve I long for, a misty veil unmasks itself in the distance, exposed by the directional shimmer of translucent golden sun rays. And it stops me in my tracks.

A halo of light pierces through the veiled façade, beckoning me forward. Light as a feather I float, my feet barely touching the ground. The force of movement is as intense as it is unwavering—like an invisible arm encircling my waist, pulling me to the light.

When I meet my destination, I am greeted by a circle of cliffs with a narrow opening. Slipping across the veil and through the entrance, my hand grazes the cool, jagged stone as I make my passage. It almost feels like the crag is alive, breathing beneath my touch.

The darkened cave within houses a mass of green. Spiny tendrils cling to the rocky surfaces, threaded with pale green flowers and red berries. And at the centre of the space, an inky pool dominates the space. Mesmerised, I stalk forward until the pool is directly below me—a seemingly bottomless well of liquid. Taking off my footwear, I dip a toe into the blackened waters. The icy sensation immediately soothes my soul. Peering into the depths, it's my own emerald eyes that float amongst the reflected images of the climbing plant.

A ripple through the water blurs the image, and a rustle from the flowers echoes as a light breeze whips through the enclave. With it, I hear a whisper. A voice, haunting and distant. Straining to make out the words, the breeze suddenly retreats, drawing the voice away with it before I can decipher them.

I wait for the longest time until the sun readies its retreat, but hear no further sound. "I'll be back," I promise to the emptiness. Because like a bird to its prey, my soul is drawn to this mystical place.

\*\*\*\*\*\*

Returning to the palace, Hermes is pacing back and forth in the entry vestibule. I throw myself into his body and wrap my arms around his waist. Then I whisper, "I'm sorry. You're right, a year will be fine."

"Come with me," he says, taking my hand and leading me toward the back of the palace.

My stomach twists in knots. Perhaps I went too far. Maybe Hermes will cast me aside—my behaviour was a little over dramatic, I guess. As we move from room to room, I realise he's taking me to the conservatory.

*He's definitely done with me.*

Sucking in a breath, I bite the inside of my cheek to

stop myself from breaking down and begging for forgiveness. Never beg—Julienne's first lesson rings through my head.

When we arrive at the conservatory, I gasp at the sight that greets me. Instead of the shattered debris I left behind, the strewn glass has been cleared. The window remains absent, but instead of the previous manicured garden vista, the space has been filled with planted red roses. Hundreds of flowers bloom in a sea of vivid ruby. And the scent is intoxicating. I'm speechless.

"Well, what do you think?" Hermes asks with a slight stammer.

"I absolutely love it." I say in awe. "I don't deserve it," I add as an afterthought.

"You deserve so much more. I'm sorry our wedding was destroyed. I promise to make it up to you, and I promise our union will be worth the wait."

"I love you Hermes," I blurt. And I think I might actually almost mean it. The internal admission plays havoc with my mind, bringing with it the image of my guide mother's disapproving scowl.

His return smile is jaw dropping. And I am reminded once again what a handsome god he is. "I love you too,

Alexandraya. Now tell me, where have you been all this time?"

The afternoon's events rush to the forefront of my mind in a kaleidoscope of images. "I've been—"

A mist of red shimmers in my vision and a finger presses to the mouth of a cloaked figure.

"... Exploring the realm," I finish.

# CHAPTER 3

## Roman

The time has come for me to leave Mount Olympus. I wish I could stay. Stay in this remarkable realm with Apollo and Siriarna. She promised she'd be back before my departure, but she's been so busy with Zeus learning to control her power that she might just forget—it seems some things remain the same, regardless of her divinity. The thought causes me to laugh out loud in the open air where I'm waiting beside Apollo's horses. They buck at the sound, joining in my private joke.

"What are you three laughing at?"

"You made it! I was sure you'd be sleeping in. As per usual," I mock.

Acteon and Lampos stamp their hooves in

appreciation of Siriarna's return. The equines are enamoured with her aura and gentle nature. I must admit, I am too.

She opens both palms displaying a golden apple in each and both horses lap up their Grand Palace treat.

"You spoil those horses," Apollo chastises on approach. "And I wouldn't want to be in your position if Hera catches you stealing her prized fruit."

"But they adore golden apples! And I'll take care of Hera if need be," she says innocently. Though the sentiment is not.

The easy banter between the two gods sends a twinge of regret to my stomach. I really do wish I could stay in the Sky Realm. However, I must return to Evolirium and continue my Propensity training. My new focus on becoming a member of The Core is unwavering.

"Are you ready, Roman?" Apollo calls.

Siriarna pulls me into a hug. In the past, I towered over her slight frame, but post her glorious transformation, she now stands slightly taller than me, "I'm gonna miss you Roman," she says ruffling my hair.

"I know you will," I say smirking up at her.

Her face crumples, she is doing her best not to cry, and

it chokes me up. "I wish I was coming with you," she says.

"No you don't. Besides, we'll see each other again soon. Friends first always," I say climbing up the ladder into the golden chariot, and blowing her a kiss.

"Friends first always," she replies. Her image soon a distant speck.

Apollo has timed our departure with the realm's sunset phase, allowing me to witness the spectacle that is Light in its purest form. My Propensity finger tingles the closer we get to the glorious yellow star.

"Would you like to set the sun, Roman?" he asks.

My throat parches at the huge honour, but I shake my head. I couldn't bear the embarrassment of failure in front of the God of Light himself, "Maybe next time." It's rather audacious assuming there will be a next time. However, I cross my fingers behind my back and send a silent wish to the Fates.

Acteon and Lampos halt their movements in position, and Apollo reaches down unhooking the lasso from its coiled position. Then he casts the golden twine in a movement that can only be described as poetic, successfully looping the celestial body.

The chariot glows, swathed in sheer brilliance as the

sun trails behind, the combination of divine objects casting tawny amber hues across the realm on the way to the vortex, and subsequently, the next realm.

Apollo's skin radiates and his hair momentarily tips white as the celestial spirit engulfs and exoduses his being. Noticing my open mouth, "It feels as it looks," he says beaming.

*Perhaps I should'nt have been so quick to dismiss his offer.*

"Magical?"

"Powerful!"

\*\*\*\*\*\*

After Apollo and I have set the sun universally, and tucked it away in its divine resting place, I am returned to Evolirium. Farewelling the great god and watching his golden chariot whirl away is tough, but walking alone in the meadows is harder. The realm has lost its allure.

Before entering my dormitory hut, I stare at Siriarna's lifeless former home and try my best not to focus on my escalating loneliness. Turning to my door, I thrust it open and enter the solitary space.

Being alone gives me plenty of time to think, and while sitting on my couch, my thoughts zigzag to Alexandraya. The last time she was here, she left her emerald pendant behind. It was in my pocket when Apollo escorted me and Siriarna to the Sky Realm after the attack on Evolirium. I had every intention of returning it to her when I arrived at her doorstep prior to my departure. But as soon as I entered Hermes palace, spite overcame righteous, and I decided to keep it instead. A memory keepsake. Or, perhaps, as a warning for future relationships. Although, if I'm honest with myself, I'm hoping Alexandraya remains unchained.

The image of her knocking on my door before the Propensity Selections resurfaces. I was hooked from that moment, love soon followed. A part of me will always love her. We were good together, and I thought our future was destined. That's before Hermes stole it. Although not a vengeful semi god, I hold a place of contempt for the messenger.

My teeth ache in response to my clenched jaw, and I refocus my energy on The Core. I plan on qualifying at the upcoming early entry trials. To do that, my skills must be matchless.

I have an edge over the other semi gods too thanks to the archaic magical tomes Apollo loaned me. After I memorised a high level-spell, he allowed me to practice under his tutelage. An absolute dream come true to any living semi god and a seldom bestowed rare gift. In fact, the more I think about it, there is no record of an Olympic God ever training a lower deity's offspring. I can't help but wonder why I had the privilege.

Yawning from travel lag, I stretch out on the couch and allow my eyelids flutter to close.

\*\*\*\*\*\*

A rosy dawn greets me, and my mood aligns with the daybreak. Whistling, I throw on my yellow Propensity uniform and jog out of my dorm hut, Zen bound.

When I arrive, the arena is empty. Moving to the light pillars, I start with the spell Apollo taught me, repeating the lines I memorised and readying my yellow Propensity finger.

"Essence of my spirited soul;
Transcend in shadow and unwhole;

22

Seize the inner Light of mine;

Hereto now this trice in time;

Create me present from within;

Project me forward in triple twin."

My precise image stares back at me from all six light pillars. When I move my hand from side to side, the reflections mirror my movements. It's remarkable. I practiced this spell in Apollo's main palace room windows, but seeing myself reflected six times in the light pillars, is next level.

"Whoa, that's tight."

Pivoting, I see Frasier, Siriarna's former Electrical Propensity member, standing behind me. "Not bad, right?" I say grinning.

"It's top tier. Where'd you learn it?"

"Apollo tutored me," I answer, god-dropping. I don't mean to sound higher than the mighty, it's just how things transpired.

His eyes widen like huge round saucers, "An Olympus God! That's unheard of."

*You're telling me.*

"It is, I agree. But I have been staying with him and

Siriarna in the Sky Realm."

He's silent for a moment. "We all thought you were in the Home Realm," he finally says, awed by my disclosure.

I'm not sure why this surprises me, semi gods don't inhabit Mount Olympus unless by express invitation and if one is lucky enough to receive such an invite, the whole realm is abuzz with chatter. "It was definitely a life changing experience."

"Wanna catch up at the Etherial Room after training today?" he says enthusiastically.

"Sure." I respond, throwing myself back into the Evolirium lifestyle.

"Great. Mind if I bring a few friends?" Fraser adds.

"Sounds like a plan." Whistling, I leave the pillars and head to my new, Year 2 Propensity classroom.

The Year 1-3 students are located in the same wing of the Learning Facility. All Propensities are separated by a section veil accessed from a central hallway. Before I reach my classroom, I run into Braxton.

*Argh.*

"When did you get back Roman? Is Siriarna with you?" he asks, his eyes darting around the hallway.

Wait, doesn't he know she's divine? Come to think of

it, Frasier didn't mention her either. Could it be that word of her transformation has not yet reached Evolirium? I toy with the idea of keeping that information to myself, but the guy looks wounded, and extraordinarily pale. "She's not coming back, Braxton."

"What do you mean?" he splutters.

"Look, there's been some developments on Mount Olympus. I'm going to the Etherial Room tonight. You're welcome to join. I'll fill you in then. Right now, I don't want to be late, I've already missed too much of the Semester and I don't want to fall behind. Especially if I'm going to make The Core."

I'm not sure why I mentioned The Core, but the look on his face is puzzled animosity. What's with that?

"Right. I guess I'll see you tonight then," he says.

# CHAPTER 4

## Braxton

Instead of attending my last Propensity class, I rush to my designated weekly meeting point. Lecturer Henrik is waiting when I arrive.

"I don't like changing our scheduled times, Braxton," he says. "It will raise suspicion and I won't put myself in that position."

*Yeah, well here he is, addicted to the nectar I'm about to hand over.*

"Sorry, Henrik, I wouldn't have changed times if it wasn't necessary."

"Right then. Don't make a habit of it."

"Have you got what I need?" I ask before handing over the prized liquid to the 320 year old semi god.

Henrik slips me a piece of paper, and I pocket it before rewarding his deception. "See you next week," he says salivating.

"Sure."

I'm looking forward to the day I can sever our association.

******

Meeting Roman at the Etherial Room is the last thing I have time for. However; if what he says is true, and Siriarna is not returning to Evolirium, I want to know why.

*Does she remember?*

Although impossible, the thought stirs panic. Forcing the wayward notion to the furthest recesses of my mind gives a much needed respite.

Taking the piece of paper from my pocket, I place it on the table, leaving it folded in quarters. I need time to digest its contents. Because unlike prior exchanges, Henrik's eyes crinkled, then glazed over when he passed this one to me.

Discarding my red Propensity uniform, I throw on a

pair of black jeans, and search for a shirt. Finding a crumpled black tee on the floor under the couch, I pull it over my head and rush out the door. I should've showered, but I've no one to impress—most definitely not fucking Roman.

By the time I arrive, he's surrounded by a bunch of Second Year Propensity students with the higher year students loitering in the background, trying to appear superior, but not willing to miss any detail.

Rumours spread fast on Evolirium, and the Learning Facility halls were rife with the news that Roman spent time on Mount Olympus. Tutored by Apollo himself. It gives him an air of superiority, and he's revelling in the attention. It grates on my nerves.

Pushing my way through the gathered crowd, I find a space next to Frasier. Knowing Siriarna was in his Propensity refreshes the wound induced by my memory. "Hey Braxton, what've you been up to? Haven't seen you around," he says.

*Probably because I haven't been.*

"Propensity training. Second Year is rather involved," I say, even though I've finished all six levels on the sly.

"Yeah. Roman is acing it though. Apollo taught him

some pretty fancy spells. Isn't that right, Roman?" he says catching Roman's attention and bringing it in my direction.

"He taught me a couple," Roman says cheerfully.

My eye begins to twitch.

"I'd love to see you in spell action," Davina says.

"Me too," Melodie agrees.

They slide into the booth and sidle up to Roman. That's when I notice the absence of Alexandraya. Come to think of it, I haven't seen her since before graduation. Usually, she completes the triangle. And she's typically hanging off Roman, swishing her hair around, attention seeking.

*Where is she hiding, and why?*

I push that question to the back of my mind. I don't really care for the answer, I'm here to find out why Siriarna hasn't returned to Evolirium. "So, Roman, what's this about Siriarna not returning?" I say, trying to sound less desperate than I feel.

The table chatter continues, and my patience crumbles like a mound of sand, "So?" I repeat.

Roman draws in a breath and I feel like jumping over the table to the other side of the booth and smacking the guy in the face. His smug expression is irritating, and my lack of sleep has left my tolerance non-existent.

"Well, she's divine," he says.

*Fuck dude, I know that. It's why I'm trying to find a way to restore her memories.*

The sound of my fists slamming onto the table causes the group to stop and stare. But before I gain the satisfaction of my fist connecting with Roman's face, Sage grabs my hand and whispers, "You're welcome," into my ear. Then she adds, wrinkling her nose, "You need a shower."

Ah, Sage. She's reversed time and saved me disciplinary action the fight would have landed me in. I should be grateful, but the pleasure of wiping that ridiculous grin off Roman's face leaves me maddened. The guy has no idea how close he came to a broken nose.

"Siriarna is a god and she'll be remaining on Mount Olympus," he further explains.

"What?" My mouth hangs open.

Roman grins in one-upmanship, "Turns out her parents are both gods."

"That doesn't make any sense," Melodie says through gritted teeth.

Now the whole table and the older years' students are in a flurry, scrambling forward keen to hear the juicy details. One of our own semi gods parented by two gods. It's unheard of.

Though come to think of it, during the rescue of Evolirium, Siriarna displayed extraordinary power in stopping the orb attack when she was supposedly Propensity-stripped. I had overlooked that truth because I was so focussed on trying to work out how to restore her memory. And, honestly, I couldn't bring myself to replay the event when Roman stepped into the chariot with her and Apollo. Of the three of them leaving the realm while I stood by powerless to stop them. I also despise Apollo— he's smugger than Roman.

"She was actually born centuries ago and frozen in time by the Fates, guarded by Goddess Eileithyia, and woken 19 years ago," Roman says, his eyes glassy at the recount.

Frasier scratches his head, and a look of confusion crosses his face, "If that was indeed the case, would we not have held a celebration ceremony and plaque presentation in the Garden of the Gods?"

Roman nods, "The news will filter through soon enough and the ceremony will take place. Trust me. She

31

was acknowledged in the Council Arena by Zeus at Alexandraya's wedding—"

His voice trails off as Mykos chokes on his drink, "Wha-what?! Who did she marry?" he splutters.

"That's the thing, she didn't. Siriarna stopped the ceremony."

"So, she's not married? Not a god?"

"No, she's not, though she is still living in the Sky Realm," Roman says, raking a hand through his hair.

I start to laugh at the irony. "So, you're telling me Siriarna is a god and Alexandraya was to become a god, but didn't, and they both reside in the Sky Realm?"

"Braxton!" Melodie snaps.

"Truth," Roman answers. And the faraway gaze that becomes him, drives me wild with jealousy.

"I want to know why Basic Siriarna was privy to her parentage. I'd like to know who *my* god parent is," Davina says, her face a wall of thunder.

Mykos' eyes squint and he takes a gulp of spiced elixir. Then, he says in a tone that is pure venom, "I want that information too. Why is Siriarna able to break the rules and get away with it?"

Mayhem breaks out as the Etherial Room is overtaken

by semi gods rioting over their heritages, predicting which god is their parent and shooting down each other's theories. Soon a fight will break out and the Realm Master will be called. I've no time for High Power Omnisensus' reprimand.

Standing, I shove my way out of the booth not bothering to say my goodbyes. Sage stands to follow, but I speed Time forward and am now sitting alone in my hut, staring at the paper Henrik gave me, willing myself to open it.

*This is it. It has to be.*

I'm almost afraid of what I may find, and it takes too many hours to work up the courage to look at the contents. Finally, with shaky hands I pick it up and unfold the note.

"Thou mind of ....... do remember past;
Sieve through Time, restore the last;
Unto all memories lost to you;
Cometh and remain heretrue;
Stay forever from hereforth now;
Accept my offer and my vow."

Below the spell is a message scrawled in Henrik's barely legible handwriting..."Braxton. From Hecate's spell book. You must conduct a blood sacrifice. By doing so, a debt will be owed to the Furies."

*Well I'll be damned. The old codger has finally come through.*

A tidal wave of thoughts crash heavily into my mind. If I do this spell, there's no going back. Do I want to mess with dark magic? Do I want to owe a debt to the Furies? Siriarna is a God, she may already be lost to me. Though I can't stand to live out the next 500 years without her knowing how much she means to me. And the love we shared. Surely that alone is worth the sacrifice? Surely?

# CHAPTER 5

## Alexandraya

The scent of melted butter, apples and cinnamon fills my senses the minute I step into the kitchen, and my stomach lets out a wild rumble. I'm ravenous after yesterday's escapade. Come to think of it, I haven't eaten since my wedding ritual.

Devouring the pancake stack in front of me, I barely taste the food, my mind peppered with memories of yesterday's discovery of Antress. That's the name I've given my secret sanctuary. It *feels* right.

"Good?" Hermes asks trailing his fingers over my lips, wiping away the dripping sweetened juice from my chin.

"Necessarily so," I laugh, licking the sticky liquid from his fingers.

He groans, his eyes hungrily staring at my lips, "Unfortunately, I have to attend an urgent divine council today."

"How long will you be absent?"

"It is expected to last until sundown."

A tingle of excitement shoots through my veins. I have a whole day to explore Antress. My eyes glisten with anticipation. Hermes mistakes the sign as distress, and rushes to my side, slinging his arms around me, "I will be as quick as I can, my love."

"Take all the time you need," I answer quickly.

He raises his eyebrows.

"I mean, I understand your enormous responsibilities in this realm. Things no other deity could possibly undertake."

He grins at the compliment. Releasing me from his grip, he tilts my chin up to his face, his hazel eyes holding my emerald gaze. Then he swoops down, pressing his lips to mine, parting them in a heady kiss of passion wanting. "I will be as quick as I can," he breathes.

My hands reach behind me, searching for something solid to steady my stance. Before I can recover from the euphoric promise, Hermes has left the palace. A shimmer of light is all that remains.

*Will I ever adapt to these sudden ethereal departures?*

Making myself a vessel of mountain tea, I take it to the revamped conservatory. Morning dew clings to the newly planted rose petals, which sparkle crimson in the rising sunshine. I draw in a deep breath and hold it in for what seems like an eternity. Julienne would be most proud of my achievement. Smiling, I release my breath, the rosy scent lingering.

A quick gulp finishes my tea, and I'm ready to set out for Antress. Bouncing through the palace to the front door, I catch a glimpse of my reflection in the entry gilded mirror and cringe. While the robe I'm wearing no longer hangs like an ill fitted sack, it looks plain and unremarkable. Perfect for a messenger, but not at all fit for a future goddess.

With a quick spell and flick of my Propensity finger, the chalky cream robe transforms into a vibrant emerald. The hue reminds me of my missing pendant and a wave of regret surges through my body. I make a mental note to retrieve it, but I refuse to return to Evolirium as a semi god.

My initial panic of not being able to find the grotto is

resolved when my feet instinctively retrace yesterday's steps—like an invisible force guiding me. As then, not a soul inhabits this part of the Sky Realm today, which only ignites my thrill of ascendency.

I amble through the narrow opening slowly, keen to savour every moment. The temperature is dramatically cooler within the enclosure, but the difference is of no bother to me. In fact, I find it exhilaratingly refreshing. Evolirium's temperature was always perpetual. No infliction, no wavering, no excitement. Antress is a welcomed reprieve.

An irresistible impulse strikes, luring me toward the glassy pool. Without a second thought, I slip out of my newly tinted emerald robe, and plunge into the icy water. The chill bites at my skin and goose bumps sting my flesh—like a watery predator taking possession of its prey. But once my body acclimatises, a sense of serenity washes through me. Sucking in a deep breath, I submerge myself below the surface.

A spontaneous bluster of wind ripples through the water, and a voice vibrates around me in the deep, "Help me—"

Unlike yesterday, today the words are clear. I strain my

vision in the murky depths to try and sight the owner, but the effort is in vain. Still, I persist. As the waves become more turbulent, my body is thrown around violently underwater. It's a warning to rise, but I remain stubbornly sunken, desperate to hear more from the mysterious voice.

"Help me. You are my only hope."

It's the sound I was hoping for. Someone *is* here. I spring off the bottom of the pool and break through the rolling waves. As soon as my head is above water, I scan the grotto for the one that belongs to the voice. Pulling myself out of the pool, I shout, "Hello, is there anyone here?"

My words fall short as the wind ebbs away, and I'm left peering into the once again whisper calm pool. Only my reflection shimmers back—the owner of the elusive voice nowhere to be seen or heard.

Shadows slither around the grotto as daylight morphs into twilight. The hours have slipped away, and it's time to return to the palace.

Leaving a trail of damp footprints behind me, I squeeze through the narrow opening, but my last step is stalled by a prickle scratching the back of my arm. Spinning around, I spy one lone tendril outstretched from its vine in what appears to be a desperate attempt to catch my attention.

Touching the delicate green flower hanging from its stem, I hear a faraway echo in the sudden light breeze, "Help me."

"Who are you?" I ask.

"My name is Smilax."

"How can I help you?" I ask in the now still aether.

There is no response. And I can't wait for one. If I don't leave now, I'll miss my opportunity to return to the palace before Hermes. "I'll be back," I whisper to the vine.

******

Psyche is waiting outside the palace doors when I return. "Ah, there you are," she says.

"Have you been here long?" I enquire, crimson tinting my cheeks.

"Not long, no."

I attempt to open the double entrance doors, but the heavy lumber is too cumbersome to shift. Psyche takes the weight and prods the doors open with her elbow as though they're as light as a feather.

40

*Gods, I can't wait to be like her.*

"Something smells delightful," she says, taking in the scent that accosts us the minute we step inside the palace.

"Come, I'll show you," I say cheerfully.

When we enter the conservatory, Psyche gasps, "Oh, it's beautiful."

"I know, I'm obsessed with it," I say laughing. Then I notice her wistful glance and my voice turns serious, "How are things with you?"

Her eyes mist and she wipes a tear away with the back of her hand dismissively. "They could be better."

Her face is tinged with grey and her wings are not as luminous as normal—the strain of her relationship clearly wearing on her body. I ache at the sight of this beautiful goddess in distress. "I'm sure things will improve soon," I say, though my voice lacks conviction. Probably because after Hermes' confession about Eros' cold behaviour, I'm not sure they will.

Though she hasn't elaborated, I know Eros has temporarily left their home due to his inability to forgive her past indiscretion—even though they weren't married at the time.

*This is Siriarna's fault.*

Changing the subject, Psyche asks, "What have you been up to today?"

Although I want to keep Antress secret, I am desperate to ask questions about the mysterious voice. "Who is Smilax?"

Psyche's wings flutter, revealing her uneasiness. "Where have you heard that name?" she asks.

I toy with the idea of backtracking, but I'm too invested to back down. "I heard it echo throughout an enclave I stumbled across."

"Be careful Alexandraya, the secret resting place of the nymph Smilax is hidden by a veil. And for good reason."

"I haven't seen her, only heard her voice," I respond guardedly.

"Of course you haven't. Centuries ago, Smilax was cursed by the Fates, and transformed into botanical form for her inappropriate love affair with a mortal named Crocus."

My mouth drops open, "The Fates turned Smilax into a vine?"

Psyche nods, "Crocus was an average mortal with high ambition. He desperately sought immortality. When he encountered Smilax on the Surface World, he plotted his way into her heart. Some say he was truly in love with her, but I am not one of them. Besotted, Smilax agreed to grant him his wish by stealing ambrosia. The King of Gods was so infuriated when he discovered Smilax's treachery, he demanded the Fates curse Smilax—a god to make is not a nymph's place. The Fates were quick to agree to Zeus' request, and transformed her into the eternal bindweed."

"And what of Crocus?" I ask.

Psyche's words are hushed, almost a whisper, "He waited on Earth for Smilax to return, only to be met by the Furies. Enraged that the Fates intervened in business they believed was their given duty, they retaliated by transforming him into a flower... after they granted him immortality. Then they returned to the Sky Realm and veiled the resting place of Smilax."

*Why am I privy to her location?*

Psyche interrupts my thoughts, "You must never return to that place."

"Okay."

"I'm serious, Alexandraya. Stay away from Smilax."

I nod my head in agreement but, deep down, I know I cannot keep that promise. I simply don't want to.

# CHAPTER 6

## Alexandraya

Hermes sweeps into the palace returning from Divine Council. His normally mischievous temperament is replaced with a pained expression, and I can't help but blurt, "What's wrong?" in a desperate tone.

"Zeus is hosting a ball in honour of Siriarna's anointment into divinity," he says, hazel eyes clouding to a storm-like grey.

My fists clench and a sharp puncture follows as my nails pierce the soft flesh of my palms. I don't flinch. "Right, I guess I'll need a new dress," I say, forcing my lips to curl upward.

Blinking, Hermes replies, "Of course love, anything

you wish."

*I wish Siriarna would leave this realm forever.*

"I want to look spectacular."

"You always do Alexandraya," he says, licking his lips.

I pick up his hand and give it quick kiss, then rub my temple, "I must rest now. See you in the morning," I say, retreating to my bed chamber.

Tonight, I want to be alone so I can plan. It may be Siriarna's anointment ball, but blending in unnoticed, is not an option. My height will be my downfall so I must ensure my outfit is impossible to miss—that *I* am impossible to miss.

******

Morning has risen and fallen five times and tonight brings with it the Divinity Ball.

Nymph Daphne tweaks the material over my left breast, "Just one minor adjustment," she says, fastening the wayward material into place. "There."

Turning to the elongated mirror in my palace dressing room, I gasp out loud. The gown is more breathtaking than I had imagined. Daphne captured my vision flawlessly. "It's perfect. Thank you."

"It was my absolute pleasure Alexandraya, I hope to see you again," she says, before slipping out of the palace as dusk engulfs the realm.

One final touch and I'll be ready to leave. Rummaging through the emerald robe in my dressing room, I reach into the pocket where I find a handful of berries plucked from Smilax on my last visit to Antress. Taking them to the powder room, I squash them between my fingers and wipe the paste across my lips, staining them bright red.

*Now, I'm ready.*

"Oh, have mercy," Hermes says as I descend the staircase.

Exactly the reaction I was hoping for. I sway from side to side allowing the light to shimmer across the silken flesh coloured material. Strategically placed vine leaves snake their way over my body and down one arm. A beaded red choker hugs my throat, and a crown of fresh red roses from the conservatory garden circles my dark braided crown.

"You approve?"

"I won't be able to take my eyes off you all night. I will be the envy of all the gods tonight." Pulling me into his arms, he buries his face into my neck and inhales, before whispering, "No one may touch you but me."

The command is provocative and highly arousing. A delicious heat spreads through my body, the warm fingers of desire settling at my centre, tightly coiled and ready to unravel. Then he slides his arms around me, running his fingers up my bare arm, and trailing them skilfully over the fabric of my dress, before pulling me tightly to his chest and taking flight. The airborne journey cools my senses in time for our arrival at the Grand Palace—my craving temporarily subdued.

Woodland nymphs usher us through the grand hallway straight to the outdoor arena, which has been transformed into an alfresco ballroom. A sparkle of stars together with a twinkle of hovering fireflies illuminates the space, and a smattering of gold dust carpets the earth below my feet. My stomach curdles as I remember my beautiful wedding and the way it was harshly cut to shreds by tonight's honouree.

Holding my head high, I step into the crowd. The gods already in attendance stop conversing to stare at my entrance, jaws dropping as the light catches my risqué evening dress. Hermes nods in passing but is side-tracked by a goddess I've not met. "Alexandraya, this is Bia," he introduces.

"Pleased to meet you," I say and smile, recognising the name of Zeus' most trusted confidant.

Bia purses her lips and turns her back while engaging Hermes in conversation.

To ease my gnawing conscious, I head straight to the beverage table and grab a goblet of wine. The earthy scented liquid hits the back of my throat and instantly warms the blood inside my veins. My breath escapes in a grateful gust.

"Well, hello there."

Spinning on my stiletto, I find myself facing Ares. "Hello."

"Care for a refill?" he says, topping up my goblet without waiting for my reply.

When I take another sip, a droplet of liquid drips from the side of my mouth. Reaching forward, Ares wipes away the spillage with his left thumb, topping up my glass with the bottle in his right—his movements precise. The skin on his fingers is rough, calloused from centuries wielding his sword.

"Thanks for your... thoughtfulness," I say.

He laughs. "Now that is something I've never been associated with."

Perhaps it's the wine loosening my tongue, but I respond without the well-practiced façade, and answer truthfully, "Me either."

Ares' eyes raise, the obsidian shining when he says, "Aren't you an exciting development."

"I aim to please," the words slip from my tongue huskily.

He grins wide, "I do like to be pleased."

I hear my name being called by Psyche. "Perhaps we'll meet again." And, I turn on my heel leaving Ares' side.

He reaches out and grabs my wrist. Tightly. The grip is almost cruel. With a twist of his lips, and a glint in his eyes as they trace over my body, he says, "I assure you we will."

My aunt's forehead creases when I join her, "Be wary of Ares, Alexandraya. The God of War is always swathed in battle, but tonight he appears more calculating than usual."

"He was perfectly charming," I reply.

"Trouble follows Ares. He cannot be reined in, not by Zeus and not by Hera. He is a dangerous god to be tangled up with," she warns.

I have no intention of being tangled up with Ares, but to say he wasn't intriguing is a lie.

Silence befalls the outdoor ballroom as a harp strums in melodic intensity. All attention is drawn to the entrance. Standing next to Zeus, is Siriarna. My eyes narrow at the same time Psyche releases a heavy-set sigh.

*Was that regret or remorse? I hope the latter because I am not ready to share Psyche with Siriarna.*

In fact, the thought makes my blood boil.

Wrapped in a golden chiton, violet sash around her waist, Siriarna steps into the ballroom, and the gods make way allowing her the room. Specks of gold dust dance around her feet with each forward step. A vortex of glitter gathers at the centre of the space before being swept up into an overhead cloud. All divine pairs of eyes are fixated skyward when the cumulous bursts, showering the crowd with golden confetti. The exhibition causes an eruption of cheer, and Siriarna is swarmed by a mass of fellow immortals.

Blood drips from the newly healed wounds in my palm as I clamp them tightly together. Psyche, spying Eros at the opposite side of the room, flutters away to join him as a droplet of my blood hits the floor.

"Here," Ares says slipping a linen napkin into my hand.

Gratefully, I take the cloth, "Thank you."

"I forgot to mention how much I like your dress," he admits brazenly.

A twinge flares at the back of my mind at the tribute, but before I answer, Hermes circles my waist possessively from behind, "There's *my* girl."

"Enjoy your night," Ares winks, and retreats.

"Was he bothering you?"

"Not at all, he was actually... thoughtful."

*Served with side of hunger.*

"Hmm, I'm sure he was," Hermes says raising his brows, and handing me some nectar.

Sipping the beverage, I'm immediately hit with the euphoric effects of the divine liquid. My mind relaxes and I rest my head against the smooth exposed torso of my partner.

Psyche returns to my side, eyes glistening in the incandescence. Eros soon joins her and slips his hand into hers. The goddess literally shimmers in response, the former glow returning to her cheeks. The four of us stand silently, but contently.

Zeus moves to the centre of the room and speaks, "Attention. As you just witnessed, Siriarna has learned to control her great inherited power. I am proud to welcome her officially into the Sky Realm and the Mount Olympus family, and rightfully hand her these keys to her own newly constructed palace."

Applause deafens the open air ballroom which, in turn, drowns out the shriek that escapes my lips.

"Thank you all for coming. I am honoured to be part of this realm and gratefully accept the key, although I will miss living in the Grand Palace," Siriarna announces demurely.

Hera, at Zeus' side—always at his side—has a plastered grin across her face. Her eyes are her betrayal—they are blank and stony. "A toast to Siriarna," she says scanning the room until her eyes rest upon Psyche.

The goddess beside me flinches but remains stalwart.

Goblets clink around the room and chatter again fills the space, celebrations peaking.

Siriarna moves through the crowd until she is standing in front of me, "Hello, Alexandraya, Hermes," she says smiling. Turning to Psyche, she extends the greeting,

"Hello, Psyche, Eros," she says cagily.

Eros drops Psyche's hand brusquely and storms off, his face a mirror of thunder. Psyche shrivels before me, her previous glow snuffed out. "This is your fault," she yelps at Siriarna before slinking away.

The scene before me is maddening, "Could you be more inconsiderate? You are still as clueless as you were on Evolirium, regardless of your divinity. In fact, it doesn't suit you at all," I say bitterly to my cousin.

Zeus and Hera join our remaining trio and Siriarna spins around to face them before speaking directly to Zeus, "Father—"

My fists ball at the reference and I can't meet Siriarna's eyes, instead I catch Hera's scowl.

"As Hermes' wedding is postponed for quite some time, it seems inappropriate to have a semi god prematurely living in this realm. Alexandraya's mortality could be of concern if we were to come under attack—"

Hermes' arm encircles my waist and he clasps my hand. Luckily, because without it, I would have launched at Siriarna. He addresses Zeus directly, "I think we could make an exception in this case. I'll ensure Alexandraya's safety."

Zeus meets Hera's steely gaze and the Queen of the Realm nods. Before he agrees, he pivots to Siriarna who holds his eye contact unwavering. Clearing his throat, he responds, "For the safety of Alexandraya, I decree her departure from Mount Olympus effective in three sunrises. Hermes, your messenger is required for upcoming duties of utmost importance, and I cannot put that at jeopardy."

I spy a smirk from Siriarna before my knees buckle. Hermes' arm tightens around my waist, keeping me vertical. "As you wish," he says to Zeus before whisking me away by winged sandals.

The next moment, I find myself in the conservatory. My scream reverberates through the space and sets flight into the open rose garden, circling the palace in a cacophonous purge. Hot tears follow. I don't bother to wipe them away, the outpour is cleansing.

"I know this is distressing, Alexandraya, but I will visit you every day. That I promise. I am eternally yours. Wed or not."

The sentiment is touching, but I feel my future is slipping away before my sodden eyes. A flash of red burns through the damp.

*Damn you to the Furies Siriarna! I will not let you destroy my carefully laid destiny.*

# CHAPTER 7

## Siriarna

Perhaps vindictive, but observing the comradery between Alexandraya and my mother causes the muscles around my heart to contract. And the belittlement of my divinity, the catalyst for my action.

I knew Zeus would agree with my request. Just as I knew Hera would oppose it. We have a strained fellowship—she tolerates me for the sake of her husband, who fawns over me. The gnarly ancient roots that bind us strengthen every day, and I am overwhelmed with his unexpected acceptance. Quite the opposite of my mother.

Things with Psyche are as sour as the spoiled strawberry tree in her palace courtyard. She hasn't forgiven me for existing—and tarnishing her reputation, and marriage, by revealing her affair with Zeus—and I haven't forgiven her for trying to kill me. We are at a stalemate. And while bitterness smears our relationship, I'm not willing to hand Alexandraya my birthright.

The year postponement of her nuptials was a clear message. But turning up tonight in that knockout dress was retaliation in its finest form. Ultimately, I had the final word.

I have my father to thank for keeping Hermes' messenger schedule chaotic. Hopefully, he will tire of the tedious realm travel and soon forget Alexandraya—finally freeing me from her meddling.

The optimism brings a smile of triumph to my lips, which is met with a glare of icy hatred as Alexandraya is whisked from the Ball in a whiz of light.

"Hello Goddess of Above. You look happy," taunts Apollo.

"Hello yourself. I am, though I'm rather weary," I reply tartly.

"Would you like chaperoning to your new palace? I've a couple of horses who need exercise!"

I can't help but laugh out loud, "Of course, if it doesn't take up too much of His Greatness' precious time."

"I will manage to squeeze this favour into my busy schedule," he winks.

How fortunate to have Apollo to lean on. Although I miss Roman, the similarities between the two are striking. It's something I keep meaning to examine more closely. Perhaps I will leave it for another day. The exhaustion of tonight's power display nestles heavily into my bones and rest beckons. "Right, let's go," I say.

******

My room teems with filtered light, indicating morning has been stretched across the Sky Realm. Today is my first waking in the new palace, bringing with it a fresh torrent of optimism. Stepping from my bed, I saunter to the windowed wall facing north, fling the casements open, and let the crisp morning air saturate the room.

My bedroom is positioned in the top turret of the modest, but striking structure. It houses elements of my dear little Evolirium hut, with three of the four walls dedicated to bookshelves. Many volumes are currently strewn across the couch. I couldn't help but read a few novels before bed to relax my mind—a much needed release last night after the confrontation with Psyche and Alexandraya.

My gaze sweeps across the woodland adjacent to the palace, and stalls at a beam of sparkling silvery light emanating from deep within the lush green canopy. Like a moth to a flame, I'm drawn to the glimmer.

Hurriedly, I pull off the loose fitting, sheer sleep tunic, and replace it with more sensible attire—form fitting pants in charcoal grey, and a simple white shirt. Much to Hera's disgust, I had an outfit fashioned in a similar style to my former Propensity training uniform, without the added armour. The casual freedom it brings feels like a warm hug, and reminds me of where my journey began.

My footsteps trample the lawn as I scurry across the soft blades of grass into the woodland. The scent of tree bark, earth, and dampened moss instantly fills my lungs.

As I move deeper into the wood, the light diminishes obstructed by towering trees, making my search for the source of the silvery light more challenging.

My journey is interrupted by an echo of song ringing through the thicket, and I follow the sweet melody, shadowing the sound. My steps slow when the vibration loudens. In the clearing ahead I spy a circle of nymphai swathed in wispy taupe fabrics, humming a lullaby. Leaning against a tree, camouflaged by spindly branches sprouting bottle green leaves, I watch, frozen in captivation.

Hands clasped, they dance and chirrup in collective harmony. And, when their moves cease and tune abates, a coppice of saplings spring to life.

The crunch of twigs beneath my feet as I shift my weight, alerts the nymphai to my presence. "Hello," I call to the deities.

Instead of responding, the nymphai let out a giggle. Then dart into the depths of the forest, collective tresses flouncing over their shoulders, beckoning me to follow. Though tempted by their lure, I decline the chase and trudge onward.

My feet travel across a carpet of velvety moss, and I slow my gait using the tree trunks as support. The texture is smooth, unlike the trees where I entered the woodland. And as I continue, their spacing becomes crowded, their trunks a deep russet. The ground beneath begins to slope, and a bough of foliage knitted together forms a barrier.

Glimmers of silver shine through small slits in the shrubbery.

*This is it!*

Heart beating wildly in my chest, I brush the covering aside, and gasp. In front of me is a floral runway, sloping downward into a hollow.

Following the trail, I reach a den that smells sweet and honey-like. Masses of snow-white flowers, with splashes of yellow at their throat, decorate the centre of the space. They are surrounded by a circular brook that serves as a natural cage.

Sunlight streams into the den through a gap in the tree canopy above, and I shield my eyes while they adjust to the brightness. When I remove my hands, the most magnificent horse I've ever seen stands before me. Its coat is a pearly alabaster; its mane and tail a waterfall of silver. Big smoky grey eyes, fringed by sooty lashes stare keenly.

"Hello there," I whisper.

The horse bucks and whinnies, then outspreads a pair downy feathered wings from its body, and flies through the gap in the canopy into the open realm.

*A winged horse?*

I wait until the hour dims, but the horse does not return. Perhaps tomorrow?

Leaving the hollow, I make quick work of retracing my

steps through the woodland to my palace—this time, no nymphs distract my passage.

As I step onto my lawn, I watch the final liquid amber glow sink below the horizon, dragging a medley of deep scarlet red with it.

Moments later Apollo knocks on my door.

"A particularly lovely sunset this evening," I say ushering him inside.

"You caught that?" he says, grinning.

"It was rather dramatic!"

"I thought it was the perfect setting for the occasion."

"And what, pray tell, is this special occasion?"

His eyes crinkle at the corners the way they do when he's about to share a premonition. "A celebration of new friendships," he says.

Curiousness sparks my enthusiasm, "Who is your new friend?"

"I'll tell you over a glass of nectar," he says, infuriatingly prolonging the details.

Over a non-discreet breathy sigh, I move to my jug of nectar and pour us both a vessel of the heavenly liquid. Apollo stifles a smile.

"Well," I say handing him the beverage.

He finally divulges, "We are celebrating your new friendship with Celeris."

"Celeris?"

"Pegasus' progeny."

The horse from the hollow. "I thought winged horses began and ceased with Pegasus?"

"So does everyone, Siriarna. Fate has led you to each other, but you must keep his existence a secret."

"I will," I promise.

# CHAPTER 8

## Alexandraya

My mind is a wreck of havoc after the Divinity Ball and Siriarna's banishment demand. The way Zeus favoured the request, despite Hera's agreement with Hermes' plea for my realm stay, was an unexpected outcome. And my looming departure is not the only casualty—Hera's control over the realm has been fractured, and the mighty queen is barely able to disguise her loathing.

*I guess that's one positive.*

After pacing the palace hallways for hours, my body weary, I finally succumb to sleep—it's a restless and nightmarish journey. In my dream I'm alone in Antress, weeping tears of blood. The dream lingers as I wake. And try as I might, I can't seem to elude the horrific image.

Hermes drags my shaking body to his, shielding me from the darkest places of my mind. "Everything will be okay," he whispers soothingly.

It takes me a few seconds to register where I am. "Of course," I reply nonchalantly. Julienne taught me to embrace and rise above adversity, and I won't let a temporary realm change dictate my carefully calculated future.

"Your strength surprises me every day Alexandraya," he says kissing my shoulders.

"And your prowess delights me," I reply in the dawning light.

Carefully, I leap from the elevated bed to solid ground, taking measured steps to the kitchen, regaining steadiness with each forward movement. Making my customary vessel of mountain tea, I proceed to the conservatory. Staring into the open space outside, the mass of ruby roses drags my thoughts back to the recent nightmare and my eyes fill with tears. I gaze at my fingers after dabbing away the moisture and I see...blood.

It's not long before Hermes is beside me, my ear-piercing scream having disturbed his peace. "What's wrong?"

I wave my fingers before his face, "I'm bleeding. My eyes are bleeding," I say, hysteria rising.

His brow is furrowed when he picks up my hands in his examining each finger meticulously. "Alexandraya, I think you'd best rest for a while."

I don't understand his complacency, but when I glance back down at my hands, there is no sign of blood. *Am I losing my mind?* "I think that might be a good idea."

Alone, I close my eyes and concentrate on meditative breathing until the midday sun shines brightly through my bed chamber window. The exercise brings clarity.

Descending the staircase, I move toward the parlour where Hermes is shuffling around. "I'm sorry, did I wake you?" he asks, his tone strained.

"Not at all."

"Are you feeling better?" he says, brows crossing again.

"Much."

A knock at the door disturbs our conversation. It's Bia. She looks to Hermes and nods and he sighs in response. Turning to me, he says, "I'm sorry Alexandraya I must leave. My presence is required at the Main Palace. I'll be back soon."

Bia laughs. "You'll be as long as you need to be."

"I understand, and I will be here when you return. Unless you are away longer than two sunrises," I say to Hermes, while glaring at Bia.

He sweeps me into his arms and draws my face level with his, then kisses me ever so gently, like I'm a delicate little bird. "I'll see you soon," he says leaving with Bia, who has not once acknowledged my presence.

I must admit, Bia's arrival, and her and Hermes' departure, is rather timely. After my earlier meditation, I knew I had to visit Antress again. For answers. For sanity. For reprieve.

\*\*\*\*\*\*

The air in the realm is still, not a wisp of breeze is present as I exit the palace and head toward Antress.

When I enter the grotto, a sixth sense hits me. A strength of connection so forceful, I'm knocked backward. I move straight to the central pool and cup a handful of water which I swallow, then I scoop another to splash over my face.

From nowhere, a gust of wind pierces through the motionless atmosphere, "I'm glad you came today."

"Is that you Smilax?" I whisper.

"Yes, Alexandraya."

"But your voice is so clear today. Why?"

"I am able to speak only through the four winds. But now you have sampled my sacred fruit, I am able to summon the winds at will when you are present."

"But I haven't sampled—"

My voice trails off as I remember the berry lip stain I applied before the Divinity Ball.

"Yes," Smilax says as if reading my thoughts.

My mind is galloping, like a chariot entering the vortex. *Can she read my thoughts too?*

"Yes! We are connected for one full rise and setting of the sun, post taste," she answers my thought.

A flash brighter than the sun at its peak hits the corner of my mind, and I am drawn into hindsight—a young and innocent nymph staring into the eyes of her partner, brimming with mirth and desire. Warmth spreads through my soul at the vision.

The bindweed's leaves begin to shake, "I knew you were the one, Alexandraya." Then she shares another vision—but this time the image is tainted. A chill shudders through me as I witness the nymph's confusion begging the Fates for her life to no avail. I *feel* Smilax's betrayal. Her heartbreak, and her hatred wind its way around my heart. Mercilessly I am overcome with such deep sorrow, I weep. "You did not deserve your fate Smilax," I say through gritted teeth.

"Do you wish to share my vengeance, and cement your desired future?"

"I do."

"You must embrace my wrath. There is no turning back."

"I am ready."

I open my heart and allow the thorny bindweed to pierce my soul. White-hot pain blinds my vision and stings my eyes. But with it comes a glimpse of my future, together with what I must do to embrace it.

Wiping my eyes with the back of my hand, I gaze down and gasp...they are covered in blood.

It is done.

# CHAPTER 9

## Siriarna

A shot of nectar hits the back of my throat, and I release a long-drawn-out sigh. The divine beverage always puts me in exactly the right frame of mind before a training session with my father. My control is steadily improving, and I'm now able to summon my power at will instead of raw emotion triggering an unruly surge of destruction. I also relish spending time alone with Zeus. When he teaches me, his demeanour changes, and I get the unique opportunity to witness a softer side of the otherwise stalwart and imperious King of Gods.

Setting down my empty glass, I pivot toward the palace doorway ready to start my stroll to the Main Palace. Out of nowhere, the gentle divine hum of power coursing through my veins bursts into an internal electric shock, and my body contorts into a strangled twist. I reach backward to the kitchen bench to steady my body. But as quick as the sensation came, it disappears leaving behind a hazy glimpse of Alexandraya veiled in red, and a sinister overtone lurking at the back of my mind.

A wave of nausea remains forcing me to stagger to the sitting room and wait for the queasiness to pass. When it does, my punctuality is sacrificed.

When I arrive at the Grand Palace orchard, sweat glistens the normal lustre of my skin.

"You're late," Zeus says tersely.

To be honest, I'm surprised he waited. Tardiness is not one of my father's tolerable traits. "I know, I'm sorry. It took me longer than I thought to recover from this morning's power anomaly."

I notice the quirk of his eyebrow, and thin pressed line of his lips. "Whatever do you mean child?"

"The electric shock?"

"Hmm I know nothing of a power anomaly. Perhaps you could sit with Hera, she'll be able to assist I'm sure," he says scratching his beard.

"It's okay father, I likely imagined it. Let's begin."

He bids a succinct nod. It's my cue. And I take it before he lectures me on time, and how *not* to waste his.

Standing tall, I summon my power and a cluster of rainclouds appear above us. I mentally direct the nimbus to quench the pear trees in front of me. But it's Hera's original golden apple tree, standing high and proud atop its own rising mound at the back of the orchard, that receives the showering. And when I realise my mistake, the downpour intensifies. Rain pelts from the increasing darkening clouds, drenching the tree, and causing the stems to loosen their grip on the prized fruit. Calming my racing heart and reining in my thoughts, I manage to control my power and cease the chaos. Clarity returns to the sky. But the ground below the apple tree is now covered in a carpet of gold—the spoils glittering in treason.

Zeus pulls at his beard. "Hera will not be pleased," he grimaces. "The consequences will undoubtedly be unsavoury—the tree takes a full calendar to produce a single fruit."

Turmoil creases his eyes and ticks his jaw. Torn by the duty to his wife, and the fledgling bond to his newfound daughter.

"It was simple mistake," I whisper, staring at Hera's wedding gift, and its barren branches.

"She will not see it that way. It's best you leave now, before she receives word."

He has taken me at face value, and I feel a swell of gratitude and the sting of restrained tears. The King of Gods, a tyrant to many, has opened his heart a crack, and allowed me a glimpse of nepotism. "I didn't mean to cause issue."

"Come now," he laughs wryly. "Your existence is issue enough."

"Perhaps I'll steer clear of the Main Palace for a time."

"A best idea."

Even though my suggestion, I wince at his quick agreement.

His face softens. "Your power is great, Siriarna. It will soon become a natural reflex. In time. Until then—"

Zeus turns, expectant at the incoming sound of footsteps, and I take the opportunity to make my retreat. Which in turn allows an escape... free from Hera, and her wrath.

******

Bia's chariot draws to a standstill beside me. "Zeus thought you might like a lift," she says, flaunting a lopsided grinning.

"How thoughtful," I mock. Though secretly, I'm delighted.

"He told me of the apples," she says feigning seriousness. Almost instantly, a surge of laughter breaks through her flimsy façade, and I can't help but join in as I pat the sacred commodity bulging in my pocket.

Our friendship was forged over the mutual mistrust of my father's wife. A friendship I trust implicitly. When the chariot arrives at my front door, I invite Bia in, but she declines. "I have another errand to take care of. Though I'll see you soon, no doubt," she says.

"Thanks for the ride."

I wait on the front porch until Bia has left, but instead of entering the palace, my eyes settle on the joining woodland, and a gentle tug pulls my conscious. With a spring in my step, I wander into the thicket. Wading through the trees, I past the coppice of saplings, merrily growing in their new environment, and continue my journey to the hollow.

The den is empty when I arrive, no sign of Celeris, but the handsome little white flowers at the centre of the space are swaying in today's delicate breeze. The hypnotic dance propels their honey-scent upward until it tickles my nose, filling it with a sweet smelling fragrance. Bending down, I notice its yellow centred throat appears to be warbling. Then, the flower speaks. "Please help me."

My head snaps back in shock, "How can I help you little flower?"

"Break my curse, set me free."

"Who are you?"

"I am Crocus."

My mind whirls into action. I know I've seen that name before. And I gulp, swallowing a mouthful of sweet tasting air when my memory serves. Crocus was a mortal cursed by the Furies for his deception, disguised as love.

My legs react automatically, pulling me upright, ready to flee the hollow. I do not possess the power to break a curse bestowed by the Furies. And even if I could, why in our gods' sake would I want to provoke a higher power?

Before I escape, Celeris flies into the lair perching himself before me. His thick sooty lashes blink while he settles his smoky gaze upon me. Reaching into my pocket

I pull out the golden apple I pocketed when leaving the main palace, and lay it flat in my palm.

*Was this morning's power slipup a divine intervention?*

Celeris doesn't hesitate, he swallows the fruit in one bite, and blows air through his nostrils.

"He was right. You are a good soul, Siriarna," the flowers speak. "It's why he signalled you. We've been waiting a long time for a worthy advocate."

I cast my mind back to the shimmer from the hollow the day I uncovered it from my bedroom window. Then, glance at the winged horse in front of me and note the way the sun's rays reflect across his silver mane and tail. "He called to me? Why?"

"Celeris has been my companion for centuries. He bared witness to my transformation and swore an oath to break the curse."

"I don't understand, could he not have approached the Fates to intervene, to restore your mortality? And why is he in hiding? The Sky Realm, in fact all realms, thought winged horses were extinct?"

The flowers begin to sway wildly, "There is no tempting Fate when Fury has struck."

I suck in a breath, "Oh."

His floral tone softens, "Celeris did not want to be stabled by Zeus like Pegasus, who never recovered after his former master, Bellerophon's, death. He is a loyal steed and has been my greatest guardian."

The equine bows his head up and down in agreement with the Crocus flowers, and stretches his neck to rest on my shoulder. His heavy breath blows my hair around my face. I giggle and stroke the soft fur of his left cheek toward his jaw and he playfully nips at my ear with his lips.

I turn and gaze deeply into the magnificent beast's smoky eyes. When I do, he projects the image of a young mortal man proposing to a nymph. The love pouring from the hallucination is overwhelming, it brings sorrow to my soul.

Celeris' memories turn from a place of joy to the depths of despair. I'm dragged into the moment the Furies arrive. The fearsome trio, hair hissing, accuse him of deceiving the nymph, and tricking her into granting him immortality—thereby breaking the divine oath. Crocus tries to reason with them, professing his true love. But the three Furies refute his claims—they wield a curse, granting the immortality he sought, but in the form of a flower.

I watch them pull red capes over their crown, turn

their backs on the flower at their feet, and disappear in a billowy haze of red.

What they didn't foresee was Celeris, watching nearby. He gently picked Crocus up between his lips and carried him to Mount Olympus where he planted the flower. Then he stamped his foot creating a divine brook, and endless supply of nutrients. In an act of benevolence, the Fates cast a veil over the hollow, keeping Crocus' resting place hidden from all immortal beings, especially their Fury counterpart.

My body is shaking at the shared memories, especially the empathy Celeris granted the mortal. My power wildly hums through my veins, and I know now I have to help Crocus. It's my destiny.

"I will help you break the curse," I say to the flower in front of me.

No more words are spoken from Crocus. Instead, the flower's yellow throats twist into a mass grin.

"Looks like I have some research to do," I say stroking Celeris' mane.

The horse neighs, and kneels down before me. As I mount, a blurred image pierces my mind and my knees buckle at its intensity. A memory bound and chained, like a prisoner begging to escape. And I can't reach it. The harder I concentrate, the tighter the shackles become. Then it's gone. However, one image unfurled and lingers... Braxton, smiling serenely at me in the Evolirium meadow.

# CHAPTER 10

## Alexandraya

My final Sky Realm sunrise bursts through the horizon without apology, and I exhale a resigned breath. Unable to sleep, I slip away from Hermes into the conservatory in the early pre-dawn hours. Staring. Thinking. Waiting. The time has come for me to return to the Home Realm.

Hermes rushes into the room and sweeps me into his arms promising to visit every moment he's not caught up in messenger duties. My heart skips a beat at his declaration of love, and I have to stop myself from wishing to the Fates to stay in this realm. They have failed me. My whole life they have failed me.

After witnessing Smilax's memories, I have nothing but contempt for the higher power. In hindsight, making my decision was easy. Stroking the berries in my jacket pocket, I smile to myself.

Hermes picks up my right index finger and slips a filigree gold band encrusted with emeralds onto it. "A promise ring," he says, his tone serious, his eyes soft.

The ring sparkles as I inspect it, casting a luminous vitreous green pattern across the remaining conservatory walls. "I just can't—"

"Shh," he says crouching down, taking my face in both his hands. "I will not let this defeat us. We are meant to be. You are my forever."

"And you are mine." I say automatically, avoiding eye contact.

He clutches my hand tightly and we trudge down the hallway, my feet dragging, bound by invisible shackles.

When we finally exit the palace, the chariot is waiting, and I'm surprised to see Iris at the helm. The Goddess of Rainbows' expression is unreadable as she throws a ladder over the chariot doorway.

Before I climb the rungs, Psyche flutters from above and stands before me. "I will see you soon," she says touching my arm with her hand.

I give it a quick squeeze.

81

From behind, Hermes' arms wrap around my waist. He hoists me into the chariot in one swift, but gentle manoeuvre.

At Iris' command the two horses take flight, and the palace below becomes a disappearing speck. Although, I catch an image in my peripheral vision; a lone horse with a rider on its back. My eyes do a double take, I'm sure I sight wings sprouting from its body, and I strain my vision to take a closer look.

But the exercise is interrupted by Hermes flying beside the chariot in his winged helmet and sandals. "I promise," he says handing me a ruby rose from the conservatory garden before floating back toward the Sky Realm.

My heartbeat hammers ruthlessly against my ribcage, and my breaths come in quick succession, "I love you." The words fly out of my mouth, and I scold myself for the emotional outpour.

Julienne's words haunt my memory, "Don't be a senseless semi god Alexandraya by getting yourself caught up in matters of the heart. It will do you no good. Love is a myth. Power is the true gift."

*Wouldn't it be nice to have both?*

******

The dip in air temperature smacks me in the face as soon as we exit the vortex. And if I'm not careful, the chilled air will permanence the scowl across my forehead. Absently, I rub my calf muscle where a faint scar remains, a perpetual reminder not to judge an enemy too quickly.

The chariot descends through the horizon and lands on the lush green lawn outside the home I grew up in, and my posture automatically stiffens in readiness. Though my legs are heavy, I force movement into my muscles, and climb down the ladder.

"A gift from Hera," Iris says, leaning over the side of the chariot and passing me a package.

The corners of my mouth lift as I take the item. "Please send my most grateful thank you."

Iris nods, shakes her reins, and the immortal horses launch into action taking flight with a compliant snort and a swish of their tails. Before they slip through the skyline, a vulture joins their departure, flying in symmetry below the underside of the chariot.

*Most unusual.*

The door slides open with sleek precision. "I'm home,"

I call out into the sterile scented mansion I grew up in. Whilst not on the same scale as Hermes' palace, it is the second largest structure in the Home Realm and signifies my guide parents' prestige.

"Lovely to see you here, darling," Julienne says meeting me in the entry, her tone curt while she scans a trained eye over my person.

"Where's Mattias?"

Julienne sighs, "Taking care of realm business."

No surprise there. As second in charge of the Home Realm, some urgent matter always needs attention, and realm business always comes first. "Of course."

"He will be back later this evening for your return dinner. In the meantime, it might be best you visit the Imperial Lake to *unwind*. Twenty minutes should do it?" she says raising her brows.

"Twenty minutes would be ideal," I say, clutching my belongings as I back out of the room. Right now, I would agree to anything to avoid the confrontation of my botched marriage. I know I'm only delaying the inevitable, but with Mattias as a buffer, I will get through the interrogation minimally scathed.

In my room, I dress in bathers and slip out the back

door without disruption. Early afternoon frost clings to the shrubbery lining the pathway, and the crisp air stings my lungs as I breathe. But I refrain from using my Propensity power, tolerating the journey to allow for acclimatisation.

Imperial Lake is deserted when I arrive. And without hesitation, I submerge myself beneath the arctic steel-blue. The sub-zero temperature almost causes my immediate evacuation, but I persevere knowing the frosty water is no match for my guide mother's wrath at an unfinished trial.

When I surface, my skin is tinged bluish-red and I'm chilled to the bone, more so than I anticipated from the twenty minute submersion. It's difficult to cast a Light speed spell through chattering teeth and numb fingers, but I persist until I'm successfully zooming home to a hot steamy shower.

Slowly the colour returns to my body as needles of scalding water burn my flesh. Ten minutes later, invigorated and reenergised, I dress for dinner, slipping Hera's gift over my black woollen dress.

"Looking great as usual, Alexandraya," Mattias says as I enter the dining room.

"Thank you," I smile aptly.

"Where did you get that?" Julienne says eyeing my red cloak.

"A gift from Hera."

My response is rewarded with a huge grin from my guide mother. "Well done Alexandraya. Well done."

# CHAPTER 11

## Braxton

Time has sped by. Mostly by my hand. Each morning I stare at the spell Henrik delivered, willing myself to speak the words. As desperately as I want to return Siriarna's memories, I wonder if by doing so, it will meddle with her divinity. That's what holds me back. Some days I throw caution to the wind and start chanting, then abruptly stop midway through the spell. And if not for this morning's meeting with the Authority, I would have projected Time forward once again.

"Good morning, Braxton," High Power Omnisensus greets, ushering me into his office.

Shuffling behind yawning, I return the greeting and slouch into a chair opposite his desk.

"I'm worried about you Braxton. Your continual manipulation of Time is affecting the realm and the other students' learning. Not to mention what it's doing to your being. It cannot continue."

"Yes, sir," I say, biting what's left of my nails.

"For your own safety, I'm afraid I have no other choice but to send you to the Home Realm for the next semester."

*Oh gods... no.*

"Please reconsider, Sir. I swear to the Fates I'll stop messing with the timeline," I plead.

My guide father's face looms before my eyes and the thought of a whole semester under Nicholas' roof triggers a ripple of shudders down my spine.

"I'm sorry Braxton, the decision is made. A chariot will collect you this afternoon. Please pack your belongings."

As the suspension sinks in, I curse myself for my recklessness. My grades have slipped and my focus on becoming a member of The Core has waned as my obsession with Siriarna intensifies. The image of her in the meadow constantly haunts my thoughts, and try as I might to block it out, I am but a slave bound to the memory.

While the Director of Students and Realm Master is a fair man, I can see by the way his jaw is set that my actions have pushed him to the limits of his patience. "Yes Sir."

"Your Propensity talents are outstanding Braxton, and you have a bright future ahead of you. Hopefully, some time away from Evolirium will help you reset and refocus, ready to embrace the final semester."

Head hanging, I leave the Authority's office, scuffling my feet as I go. In a daze, I almost run into Henrik. "Hi Henrik. How's it going?" I ask, straightening my posture.

"Fine, Braxton. Fine," he says stuttering as he notices the Authority behind me.

"Good to hear," I say finding some joviality at finally being free of the seedy lecturer, and his greedy nature.

Henrik bows his head, avoiding further eye contact, and scurries down the hallway. I leave in the opposite direction.

Placing my Propensity training on hold is sufferable as I'm already covertly skilled at a Year 6 level. It's living with Nicholas that has my jaw clenched so tight it aches.

When I reach my dorm hut, my mood is palpable. Mumbling to myself, I rip my satchel from its hook, and throw a few shirts from the floor into it, together with items I don't dare leave behind, and slam the door shut after me.

Instead of heading straight to the chariot, I make a detour at the meadow and lay amongst the clover and close my eyes. Then I freeze Time, holding the Evolirium ribbon tightly in my palm.

*No point in worrying about the consequences, I'm already suspended.*

Images of Siriarna dance before my eyelids. Her face, so angelic and full of wonder below me. Her skin, luminescent and silken beneath my touch. Her lips, full and soft against mine. The memories slash at the depths of my soul, and my heart wedges itself in my throat. Swallowing the misery of what was lost, my focus loosens and my grasp on the Ribbons of Time slips.

Roughly I swipe at my eyes with my stained shirt sleeve, and trample the clover in a hasty departure. My feet slap roughly at the pathway, the sound diverting my thoughts to the Home Realm and what lies ahead.

Approaching collection point, I run straight into Roman.

*For fuck's sake.*

"Where are you going?" he says noting my satchel and

the stationary chariot ahead.

"The Home Realm," I say sidestepping and moving closer to my ride.

"Why?"

*Oh for the love of gods'...* "I need a break from here," I huff.

"You'll miss The Core trial."

"I'll catch it next time."

He squints his eyes, and then shrugs. "Your loss."

"You have no idea," I snap and board the chariot.

******

Every ounce of grit is needed to confront Nicholas, which is why I instructed the chariot to land in the green space at the southern end of the Home Realm, three squares from my guide home.

Now, I'm wandering as slow as physically possible toward the next three months of punishment, stopping momentarily by the Imperial Lake. Here, I observe a body floating below the surface of the icy lake. Ripping the shirt from my body, ready to dive into a rescue, I witness jet black hair swirl in time with ballet-like arm movements.

Emerald green eyes open beneath the surface, and I duck out of view before Alexandraya can recognise me.

*What in the gods' name is she doing?*

Without a second thought, I expertly cast my spell and freeze Time for several moments.

Whistling, I jog home.

Paulette is in the kitchen when I try to slip into the house. "Braxton, I'm so happy to see you. Although we need to chat about why you're here, in detail—"

"Sure Paulette, I'll just put on a shirt," I interrupt.

"Go on now. Maybe take a shower—you look terrible by the way," she says, ruffling my long greasy hair.

Much as I hate to admit it, perhaps the Authority was right in sending me Home.

"You look like shit," booms Nicholas as I pass through the kitchen.

Then again, maybe he wasn't.

# CHAPTER 12

## Alexandraya

I gaze feebly at the rose Hermes gave me as the last petal tumbles to the floor. Fourteen sunsets have befallen since my Sky Realm departure. And though I try my best to suppress the rising fear of abandonment, the containment is proving difficult. As is the foreign erratic heartbeat that is plaguing my chest.

Yet another day slips away with not an utterance, and I fall into a fitful slumber where my dreams taunt me— images of my wedding day, and the fateful moment Siriarna stole my future.

*Gods I despise her.*

When I wake, Julienne is standing over my bed. It used to startle me, sometimes a scream would follow, but years of practice has me unflinching. "Good morning, Julienne."

She doesn't smile. "You were screaming in your sleep."

"I had a nightmare."

"Tell me about it," she says sitting at the end of my bed.

My skin prickles at the loitering vivid night-memories. "I dreamt of Siriarna ruining my wedding."

Julienne's normally emotionless face cracks, lines appearing at the corner of her eyes. "We do not allow for defeat, Alexandraya. This isn't over. It's your destiny."

"What if he's forgotten me?" I whisper, unable to hold back the words.

"Then you haven't executed your task properly."

"I-I'm sorry."

"Self-pity is a sign of weakness, and it doesn't suit you. Time to dig yourself out of the mess you've created. Besides, there's more than one available god, Alexandraya," she says shrewdly. "We will concentrate extra hard on your trials tomorrow." The edges of her mouth lift a smidgen, her lips moisten, then part. But instead of speaking, a faraway euphoric expression crosses her features, and a twinkle lingers in the corner of her eyes.

I toy with telling her about Smilax and our plans, but I

know better than to answer. Instead, I simply nod. The action appeases my guide mother, and she leaves my room in a waft of happy distraction.

Fleetingly, I think about burying my head under the covers. However, I force myself to kick off the toasty warm blankets—much to the disgust of my body that groans in protest.

The daily trials, each one more intense than the last, are excruciating, and every muscle in my body aches. Today will be no exception. In fact, it will be gruelling after this morning's transparency. So, I dress in a pair of training pants and a tee that I knot at my chest, and casually make my way downstairs, coolly composed.

By the time I reach the kitchen, piles of pancakes and fresh fruit laden the table. The sweet-smelling aroma fills my nostrils and my stomach growls while my mouth begins to salivate. I'm starving after the rigorous training I've put my body through these last two weeks, and the lack of nutrients is beginning to take a toll.

"Morning, Alexandraya," Mattias says brightly before shovelling a fork full of pancake into his mouth.

"Morning, Mattias."

"Are you going to keep staring at that food or are you

going to tuck in?" he winks.

I sneak a quick glance at Julienne who is pouring herself a mug of freshly brewed rose petal tea. "I'm not hungry today," I reply.

She flashes me an approving grin.

*The trial of abstinence—my least favourite trial.*

"I'm off for a run, I'll see you both this evening."

"As you wish dear," Julienne replies.

Mattias' hearty farewell, along with the echo of humming, tarries as I flee through the back door.

The realm is chilly, and I allow myself to run without using my Propensity power—it distracts my stomach from its aching hunger. My feet slap at the pavement in a steady rhythm and the tension in my body begins to ease. A run was exactly what I needed.

By the time I reach the outer skirts of the realm, sweat clings to my skin and my breathing is heavy, signalling that it's time to take a mini break. Sitting in the grassland I unclip my water satchel and take precisely one sip.

When my breathing returns to normal, I reach into my pocket and retrieve a bindweed berry. Then I place it on my tongue and swallow with my second sip of water.

"Hello Alexandraya. How are you?" Smilax's voice fills

my head.

"I'm afraid I have bad news. No word from Hermes, and no set return to the Sky Realm," I say agitated.

"You will—"

Footsteps approach from behind. "Who are you talking to?"

My head snaps around and I find Braxton standing there, looking far less appealing than I remember. My communication with Smilax is broken by my lapse of concentration.

"Myself," I reply brusquely. Followed by, "What are *you* doing here?"

His eyes are wild when he answers, "Taking some time to refocus."

"I see," I reply narrowing my eyes.

"Aren't you supposed to be living on Mount Olympus... with Siriarna?"

His attempt to mask the pain in his voice when he mentions her name is admirable, but feeble. "I will be returning soon enough," I smile sweetly.

"You sound less confident than usual," he says snidely.

*I must be off my game.*

Though Braxton has always been difficult to

manipulate, the one semi god who is completely immune to my charms. And I have never bothered to wonder why that is. Through my wince, I catch a reflection in the corner of his eye, a glimmer of red. "Well Braxton, if you must know, Siriarna thought it best I return to the Home Realm while I wait for my upcoming wedding. Personally, I believe she didn't want anyone interfering in her relationship with Apollo. He really is quite taken with her."

Without a word, Braxton retreats, muttering something under his breath.

*Judging by the sheer malevolence shining through his eyes, I have succeeded.*

Congratulating myself on hitting the right nerve, I take my third sip of water—which I almost choke on as the ground around me quakes.

Four striking horses, bridled in gold, thunder into the grasslands, Ares at the chariot helm. He slings his legs over the side, dismounting aggressively, and comes to stand before me. "Alexandraya, I've come to make sure you are alright." A hint of practiced sincerity plagues his tone— similar to the one I, myself, have perfected.

"Yes, I'm fine. Should I not be?" I say offhandedly.

He places his tanned, calloused hand lightly on my shoulder, "I thought you may need a friend now that Hermes has found another."

My breath catches and my heart sinks, but I ensure my face remains calmly neutral when I reply in an even tone, "Thank you. I'm fine. Though I do fear you've wasted a realm journey."

"You could never waste my time, Alexandraya. Please let me help you navigate this difficult time."

His words are a contradiction to his sly actions. The way his eyes expertly scan my form in practiced battle assessment, thwarted by the rise of his brows when his vision stalls at my lips—battlelust.

Julienne's words ring through my ears, "There's more than one god." Warmth spreads through my body and I'm careful not to let the jubilation spread to my face. Tilting my head to the God of War, I say, "I was about to make my way home. Would you care to accompany me?"

"I would be delighted," Ares replies.

# CHAPTER 13

## Braxton

*Apollo. Fucking Apollo!*

No—I don't believe it—I won't. My brain is nothing but a hot mess of confusion, a rollercoaster of plunging emotion. Images of Siriarna in Apollo's arms mock me while the voice in my head lures me toward the memory spell. No chains of reason hold me back, and I scramble from the grasslands to return home.

The house is empty when I arrive, and while my throat is parched, I bypass the kitchen heading straight to my room in search of my prized possessions. Hunting through my satchel brings no success. The spell is not where I left it, and neither is Siriarna's amethyst pendant. My face flames and beads of sweat prickle my forehead as

I tear the satchel to shreds, hoping the items are secretly held captive by the textile.

"Looking for these?"

Nicholas is standing in my doorway taunting me with both the pendant and the spell.

"Give them back."

"Now, boy, why would I do such a thing? These could bring me many favours," he says smugly.

"They don't belong to you," I stammer, the heat draining from my face, the sweat running cold.

"I think you've got some explaining to do, boy. These items are tremendously coveted. The pendant alone is worth a fortune and the spell... well, that is almost priceless."

I raise my palm and chant, ready to reverse Time and reclaim my belongings. But the ribbons do not come to hand, and I falter. A throaty chuckle echoes around the room. "You should know me better than a fool Braxton, your powers will not work within this realm—I have bound your magic—"

"You asshole."

Nicholas' jaw ticks, an indication I've gone too far. He steps forward quickly, fist positioned to strike. At the same moment Paulette passes my room, witnessing the first punch. She shrieks and rushes toward me. My hands raise in desperation, motioning her not to enter. But it's too late, she's kneeling on the floor space in front of me inspecting my face. That's when Nicholas' knee slams into her cheek sending her ricocheting across the room. She swallows a scream, but the wince betrays her bravery. Purple begins to streak her face, and a flash of red burns my pupils as I stare at the back of my retreating guide father.

Paulette's eye is swollen shut and needs lancing to release the pressure. Shame hangs my head, as I scurry to retrieve the first aid kit stashed in my armoire. "I'm so sorry Paulette," I say holding her hands, burying my face between them.

"It's not your fault, sweet," she says soothingly. The words send me spiralling back to my childhood.

"I am supposed to take care of you, and I have failed," I whisper.

"I'll have none of that Braxton. I'll be fine momentarily. It's not your job to take care of me."

It's true, physically she will heal quickly—a perk of being a semi god—however the damage will remain, burned forever in her mind's eye. "You wouldn't be injured if I wasn't here."

"Nonsense—"

She stops mid-sentence, and our eyes meet. Without a further word, I tilt her face, incise her wound and daub the drainage.

"Thank you."

There's so much I want to say, but I already know the answer to the question I have begged too many times to count. Instead, I drape my arm around her shoulder, and manoeuvre Paulette to the cosy sitting room nook where I settle her into the wingback armchair, adjusting the cushions behind her back. "I'll be right back."

Although I am rewarded with a smile, I note the effort behind the forced upturn of her mouth, and the drip of blood that seeps from her right eye.

*One day, I will stop him.*

In the kitchen, I pour two glasses of spiced elixir, and stir a spoonful of valerian root powder into Paulette's. I may not have my magic, but the herb will soon see my guide mother resting peacefully.

"Here you go, Paulette," I say returning to the sitting room, handing her the beverage, and a cloth wipe.

A resigned breath escapes her lips as she sips the warming liquid, and mops her eye. "How is your jaw?" she says her voice faltering.

"It's alright. Don't worry about me, just you rest."

"I'm glad you're home, Braxton," she says though hitched breaths.

"It's great to be here, Paulette," I say smiling. Although I can't say I'm thrilled to be living under Nicholas' roof once again.

Mist wells in her untouched eye, and she blinks briskly while taking another sip of her drink. Thanks to the herb, it's not long before my guide mother is sleeping soundly. Tucking a blanket around her body, I bend down and kiss the top of her head—"sleep well Paulette," I whisper.

Knowing Nicholas will spend the evening at the seedy gentlemen's club in town, no doubt cunning a deal for Siriarna's pendant and Hecate's spell, makes my blood boil. If I don't act quickly, the items will disappear, forever lost in the depths of the shadow market.

Flashes of red pierce my mind like bubbling lava, propelling me toward the door. Gulping my elixir in one mouthful, the spice hitting the back of my throat, I am ready to salvage the items that belong to me.

Each step I take from home is deliberate and forceful. Without magic, every ounce of wheeling and dealing Nicholas unwittingly taught me, will be required.

Cutting through the grasslands to town, I am confronted with Ares' war chariot abandoned mid field. Its four horses leisurely nibbling on surrounding blades of grass. They ignore my presence and continue to munch while my eye catches a glint in the chariot. The gleaming red enamel seduces me like a fiery beacon of hope, luring me closer.

Springing from the ground, my hands reach out to grasp the lower chariot rail, limbs dangling below swinging back and forth until the momentum hoists me into the chariot. Standing at the helm, I reach for the reins and inspect the fine leather, slackening them in my palms. The heightened vantage point allows me to gaze straight toward town, and the gentlemen's club comes to view in the twilight. My hands unconsciously squeeze the reins as flashes of Paulette's purple cheek re-emerge. It's enough to trigger the horses into action. After rearing on their hind legs, all four begin to canter across the grasslands at the misguided instruction. It won't be long before they're airborne.

"Easy does it," I command, pulling back on the leather with all my muscle. But the order is useless, and the horses bolt onward trampling the earth below, kicking a mixture of dirt and grass pollen into the air. I'm tempted to abandon chariot and hurl myself over the side rail, but instinct keeps my grip firm and my stance steady.

As the edge of the grasslands approaches, I squint my eyes semi closed, poising myself for flight. Overhead a vulture squawks in a low and guttural vocalisation, and the horses immediately relax their furore and halt their ride.

*Thank the gods.*

The vulture circles and swoops in my direction, its wings flapping furiously. I can literally hear the beats of my heart pumping as the bird approaches—oh my gods, it's coming at me. For the second time today, I'm going to be struck.

Raising my hands in defence, I hear the hiss of the bird, and smell its rotten breath, before one of its razor sharp talons scrapes down my right palm slicing open the flesh. A savage scream belts out of my mouth, and I dive under the belly of the chariot.

Under the relative safety of my shield, I rip the bottom

of my shirt with my uninjured hand and wrap the material around my injury. The predator hovers above, my blood staining its sharp, hooked beak, beady eyes pinpointed in my direction.

*Where did it come from? There are no vultures in the Home Realm.*

As if reading my thoughts, a hollow squawk pierces the air and the vulture soars into the sky. I seize the opportunity to crawl from my hide, and bolt from the grasslands.

Instead of attacking, the bird flies overhead in the same direction, like a lethal feathered spirit guide spanning an otherwise lifeless horizon.

By the time I arrive at the club, twilight has turned to dusk. A chorus of drunken roars blasts through the crack in the entrance doors as does a haze of cigar smoke. The club is rowdy this evening, a forewarning that the best way to slip inside unnoticed, is through the service entry.

As I make my way down the side passageway to the service entrance, my palm begins to throb. Moisture soaks through the makeshift bandage, dripping to the ground in sticky red clots.

Trance-like, I glare at the sky where the vulture hovers,

and in an instant it plummets downward, the squall from its wings slapping my cheeks. Instinct kicking in, I chant to freeze Time. And to my complete surprise, ribbons appear in my bloodied palm.

Perched directly in front of me, the vulture blinks its eyes almost closed revealing its third eyelid, allowing my vision to tunnel into its soul.

*Ares?*

With a toss of its head, the vulture scrapes its wings across my wounded palm and journeys skyward, disappearing from view.

All the while, the Ribbons of Time remain intact and stagnant. With a slight tremor, I twist the Home Realm's ribbon and reverse Time a few seconds. The vulture returns to earshot. "Thank you," I voice in bewilderment, the whole turn of events scrambling for sense in my brain.

The bird resumes its retreat without hesitation, and Time returns to normal pace. I can't quite understand why the God of War would assist my power return, though his lust for bloodshed is well documented. Perhaps he bore witness to my inner fury?

Nevertheless, a smile spreads wide across my face... it's time to reclaim what's rightfully mine.

# CHAPTER 14

## Alexandraya

The stroll home to my guide parent's home with Ares is somewhat cathartic. The flirting distraction is welcomed after discovering Hermes' abandonment. And Ares is open to my charms—he is attentive and responsive—laughing at my well-practiced witticisms, and eyeing my body openly each time I giggle. It would seem the God of War is the perfect divine replacement.

"Thank you for escorting me home, Your Great," I say, fluttering my eyelashes.

His eyes are raised when they focus on mine, "I think we are past formalities, Alexandraya."

"As you wish... Ares," I say tilting my head in a way that allows a cascade of silky hair to fall across my face.

He reaches forward and tucks the loosened strands behind my ear, "That's better." His tone is as fierce as it is flirtatious.

"I appreciate you coming to the Home Realm to check on me."

"You left an impression, Alexandraya. I believe our paths have crossed for a reason. And I believe you are destined for the Sky Realm."

His words are harmony to my ears, a sonata of seduction, and I clear my throat demurely to hide the squeal of delight threatening to escape. "I feel the same connection," I lie.

He takes my hands in his, "May I call on you again?"

"I would very much like that."

He brings my hands to his lips and kisses the back of them firmly, gnashing his teeth across my skin, drawing a fine line of blood. His hardly contained delight escapes in the form of a growl, and I suppress the triumph building in my stomach. "I'll be back at midnight on the full moon," he says, and retreats from my door. His shadow soon becomes a distant speck, replaced by that of a vulture careering into the sky.

*Indeed, I am worthy prey. But beware the huntress whose*

*flesh is tainted.*

******

Inside the sanctuary of my room, hugging my arms around my body, I replay the afternoon's revelations.

A knock at the door interrupts my thoughts, and Julienne surges into my room without invitation. Her stance is rigid, and her voice is terse, "Where have you been? I thought we were parading through town on our way to sit with the Realm Master for a briefing mid time today? I had to attend alone and explain your absence, which was nothing short of embarrassing, Alexandraya. Mattias won't be happy."

"I was delayed due to an unexpected meeting with Ares," I say god-dropping, playing my ace.

Her face relaxes at the news and she moves to my bed. She collects the brush from my dresser on her way, and begins to comb through my hair in long even strokes. "Oh, what lovely news, tell me all."

I exhale a long breath and retell the meeting between Ares and myself. Whilst I mention Hermes' rejection, keeping my voice as calm as one of my well-practiced emotion free elocution lessons, I emphasise the conversation that played out between Ares and myself, his marking of my skin, and the promise of further trysts.

"He sounds well on his way to falling for your charms my girl. I am so proud of you. You *will* become the god you were born to be."

"Thank you Julienne, your tutor has served me well."

"I'll be right back," she says, leaving the room.

When she returns, she is carrying a small vial of golden liquid. "Here, this will seal your ultimate success," she says handing me the fragrance.

I open the vial and the scent that escapes is strong and heady. A mix of pungent earthy aromas finished with a blend of exotic woody top notes. It's intoxicating. "Oh my gods." I gasp.

"Exactly," Julienne laughs.

"Is this not divinity itself?" I breathe out slowly, letting the scent linger as long as possible. "What is it?"

"Frankincense. Ares will not be able to resist. I have been saving this for the perfect moment and, Alexandraya, this is it," she says giddy.

Licking my lips in keen anticipation, I recork the vial and place it carefully on my bedside table. It positions next to the deceased rose that Hermes bestowed—I have not had the will to dispose of it. Nor did I need frankincense when I was with him, come to think of it.

Julienne catches the faraway expression and scoops up the strewn rose petals, together with the vase its barren stem inhabits, and walks wordlessly from my room.

My heart squeezes at the loss of such triviality, and I wonder how I let myself fall prey to its traitorous beat. Placing my hand across my chest, I vow to not make the same mistake with Ares.

Popping a bindweed berry into my mouth, Smilax's voice floats into my mind. "Hello, Alexandraya."

My thoughts transcend instantly, "I have found a divine replacement. The God of War has fallen into my lap." I can't help but smile at my twist of fate.

"How fortuitous. He will be the perfect substitute before the war begins," she says.

The threat of war does not shock me as it should. In fact, I relish the chance to unleash the simmering rage that's pent-up inside my body, begging for release. I need the euphoria bought about after a power surge. It's been way too long. "Who will be at war?" I add as an afterthought.

"That I cannot disclose, however, this battle was forged in the dark ages, and I have been waiting for too many centuries for it to arise."

I can taste the bitterness in her voice, and once again am reminded of the circumstances that led to her transformation from woodland nymph to bindweed.

My jaw clenches at the memory. And I know at once the greatest war of our history is about to reign forth.

A flash of red sprouts before my eyes signifying my allegiance, and clarity abounds. The significance of Hera's gift unfolded. Sides are chosen. I am glad of mine.

A battle of Fury vs Fate.

# CHAPTER 15

## Braxton

Arms stretched forward, I shove the back door open with all my weight, and barge into the gentlemen's club. My sight is set on the corner booth behind the bar where Nicholas conducts his shadow market business.

Despite the hostile stares from the rowdy crowd, I move through the club to my target. A mid aged semi god, thickset in build, grabs my arm, "This is no place for a youngen," he slurs, halting my passage.

Snarling, I reply, "I'm able to take care of myself."

He peers at my overgrown hair, blackened eye sockets, and then shakes his head and laughs. "I highly doubt that."

"Let me show you," I taunt, summoning the Ribbons

of Time to my palm and seizing the Home Realm ribbon between my thumb and forefinger.

Glaring open mouthed at my power on show, he stutters, "No need to mess with Time here." Then slinks backward, disappearing into the raucous crowd.

Releasing the ribbon and my clutch on Time, I continue with dogged determination toward the booth. The smarmy sound of his laugh echoes as I approach and alerts me to the deal Nicholas is about to close. It's his tell. And one I have become well accustomed to over the years.

He turns before I reach the table, a bemused grin spread across his face, although when he speaks his eyes narrow to slits, "What are you doing here?"

"I've come for my items," I say matter-of-factly, staring at the opened display box housing both pendant and spell.

"Excuse me gentlemen," he says to the men sitting in the booth opposite.

These men are definitely not gentlemen—big, burly and shrewd, nothing about their presence is gentle.

Nicholas slaps his hands on the table and stands over me exhaling a cloud of cigar smoke into my face, "You mean, *my* items. Now, go home, Braxton, I've no time for this pointless disruption," he drawls.

The men at the table belly laugh. "You tell him Nicholas," the elder man says roughly. "Get lost youngen, before I make you."

"There'll be no deal today," I say calmly. Then, I turn to Nicholas, "I'll take my items now."

His jaw ticks, and he takes a step closer, "Leave, Braxton," he sneers.

Drunken cheers echo around the booth and a crowd draws at the commotion. With a showdown looming, Nicholas poises his fists ready to strike. He is lapping up the attention from the horde, their jeers spurring him on—a swagger of ammunition. Not that he needs an added validation for violence.

In response, I summon the Ribbons of Time to my palm, and begin to chant.

"Wait... what are you doing? Your powers are bound," he says paling at the sight in front of him.

"Obviously not."

I allow myself a second of triumph at his horror-struck expression, and then freeze Time. With the room silenced I take my shot and connect my clenched fist with his jaw—payback—then I swing again, this time at his cheek—payback for Paulette.

Nicholas' face is blank as he comes to. He scans the room and notes the rest of the club's patrons are Time frozen. His eyes widen as the realisation sinks in and then his hands fly to his cheek, "Your power—"

"It's impressive, right?" I say, smirking in victory at the cower lurking in his voice. With an ice calm tone I add, "You will never touch me again, nor will you lay a hand on Paulette. If you do, I'll kill you, Nicholas. I swear to the Furies, I will kill you."

The venom in my words causes his eye to twitch but he remains silent. Reaching down, I take the pendant and spell, turn my back on my guide father, and whistle while I walk from the club.

The adrenaline pumping through my veins is exhilarating. Patting my pocket where the box is secured breaks me out of the glum I have been flailing about in since Siriarna left Evolirium.

Thinking about her sends my heartbeat into overdrive. And I know I'm powerless to stop the inevitable—I will be using the spell. For my sanity. Regardless of the consequences, I cannot fight my conscious any longer. I've wrestled with it too long.

Coincidentally, I arrive at the grasslands, eerie and

vacant at this hour. Silvery streaks illuminate the fields and the reeds dance in harmony to the melody of the delicate breeze. A lone black feather tipped with ivory lays in a divot left behind by Ares' chariot. It gleams beneath the moonlight—a contradiction of light and dark.

*Time is present. I must mend the past. To right my future.*

Goosebumps prick my flesh as I take the box from my pocket and gingerly remove Hecate's spell. Henrik's notation about a blood sacrifice catches my eye, as does the purple wound in my palm.

Briefly, I wonder if the debt I'll owe is worth actioning the spell. Then I chant, clear of conscious...

> "Thou mind of Siriarna do remember past;
> Sieve through Time, restore the last;
> Unto all memories lost to you;
> Cometh and remain heretrue;
> Stay forever from hereforth now;
> Accept my offer and my vow."

Picking up the vulture's feather at my feet, I slice my palm across its earlier laceration to release my blood. As the droplets splatter onto the paper, the spell begins to burn until all that is left is a plume of dusky smoke. The haze fills my lungs and scorches the fibres as I breathe in. Despite the searing pain in my chest and the threat of passing out, I keep inhaling until every waft is ingested, all the while fighting not to release the building scream perched at the back of my throat.

Sacrifice accepted.

An invisible weight settles onto my shoulders, and I adjust my muscles to compensate the burden. While the physical load is much to carry, the heaviness in my heart has been released.

*My gods, it worked.*

Immediately, my thoughts are filled with images of Siriarna, and I can't stop smiling. Finally, endless exasperating days of searching, wishing, and bargaining have ended in triumph. My eyes sting as my soul is set free. *"Almost free,"* an internal voice cautions. But even the inner warning cannot extinguish the delight of a promise fulfilled.

Time to prepare.

Time to reunite.

Time to get out of this realm.

My body responds and my feet trample the earth below. At the edge of the grasslands I find Alexandraya sitting, staring wistfully at the sky. Against better judgement, probably due to my current elation, I stop and ask, "What are you doing here?"

"I'm waiting."

"Ah, right. Good luck with that," I say with a renewed sense of cheer, and pivot to continue my journey home.

She grabs my arm, emerald eyes twinkling mercilessly in the moonlight, and says, "You know we are the same, Braxton."

Reaching down I remove her fingers from my arm and notice her normally sharpened nails are bitten to their beds. "We are nothing alike, Alexandraya."

"Are you sure?" She smirks haughtily.

I have no time nor desire to spend another second in her company. "Absolutely."

"Sometimes a sacrifice, no matter the reason, is all it takes for enemies to unite," her voice purrs.

I'm jolted to the spot, literally unable to move.

*How does she know of my sacrifice?*

My nonverbal response is enough for her to continue,

"Fury spreads like wildfire," she laughs, then lightens

the starless night sky with a beacon of red.

My chest burns as her Propensity Light carves a menacing fiery streak through the sky and unable to stand the heat, I tear off my shirt.

Her eyes lock on my scythe tattoo, and she raises her eyes before speaking, "As I said Braxton, we are the same."

My ebony inked scythe tattoo is now surrounded by a blazing red line.

*What have I done?*

# CHAPTER 16

## Siriarna

The silvery moonlight pouring through my bedroom window indicates another day has slipped away. And I am no closer to breaking Crocus' curse. The frustration is maddening, but I uncurl my legs from the floor and pad my way carefully through the strewn novels to my bed, where I fall asleep as soon as my head hits the pillow.

When I wake, I don't feel even the slightest bit refreshed. Instead, I'm left with a twinge scratching the back of my mind—a subconscious headache.

Shaking off the slumber hangover, I pull on a pair of sleek white riding pants and a simple malt coloured wraparound shirt in preparation for today's requested meeting with my father.

Leaving the palace for the first time in days, the brilliant glare of the sun stings my vision as I step into the light. Walking past the woodland that hugs the perimeter, I am lured closer by the lilting sound of beating wings. Hidden between the speckled grey tree trunks, and mossy undergrowth, is Celeris.

"Hi, boy," I say, joining him in the thicket.

He whinnies, and bares his teeth.

Laughing, I stroke his mane, and coo, "I'm heading to the Grand Palace now. I mustn't be late."

He bobs his head, and flutters his nostrils blowing air across my face. The warm horsey breath takes no mercy, whipping my hair into a matted mess, and leaving me no time to remedy it.

Smoothing the strands as best as I can, I kiss Celeris on his muzzle, and dart from the forest to my lawn. When my escort arrives, she takes one look at my hair and raises her eyebrows.

"I know, I know," I say, raking my hands through my hair again.

"You know I like you just the way you are, right?" Bia says, laughing.

"Remind me again why?"

"You provide much entertainment. Not to mention raw courage. Perhaps I'll sneak you into the palace through the western side entrance?"

My father's most trusted messenger has saved me more than once from the wrath of his wife. "Thanks but that isn't necessary."

"Feeling brave are we, Goddess of Above?" she quips.

"I wouldn't want to rob you of your amusement!"

"As you wish. But don't say I didn't warn you."

As expected, Hera answers the door when I arrive. She gives me a slow disapproving scowl. But it's not the grimace that catches my attention, it's the blood red cape she's wearing. A feeling of déjà vu strikes, and my pulse begins to speed. "Hello, Hera," I say, forcing a smile.

"Siriarna, your presentation needs work. You are a *goddess* and we have exacting standards," she berates—her face a special kind of sour—reserved just for me. She runs her eyes over my flushed cheeks, and lingers her gaze on my hair. "You look like a woodland nymph. And before you say a word... that is not a compliment," she says retrieving a twig from my wayward hair.

Bia's chuckle is in earshot.

My scathing retort is left unspoken as Zeus appears.

"Ah, Siriarna, you're here. Good, good. Follow me."

I flash Hera a lip curling smile and raise my brows, "Wonderful to see you... as always," I say smugly.

The shadow she casts from her cape as she pulls the blood red hood over her head, drains the wit from my soul as if sucking it dry. And I swallow wildly to keep it at bay.

Hera's quick pivot almost disguises the attempted reaping, but I catch her smirk in the shiny marble floor.

*A warning shiver prickles my spine.*

Shaking off the premonition, I hustle after Zeus. He strides through the palace reaching his private den, and positions himself behind the imposing wooden desk. The leather inlay carved into the timber is highlighted by a stream of filtered light that shines through the spherical window above it—functioning like a natural spotlight. The rest of the den is dim and sombre. Seamlessly integrated bookshelves line the walls and house original tomes, parchments, and realm maps. The sight of such historical information makes my mouth water.

"Come in, Siriarna. Sit down. Is your power causing you distress?" he says, brows knitting together.

"No, my power is fine."

Lingering by the bookshelves, breathing in the scent

of their knowledge, I notice my father swipe a piece of parchment atop the leather inlay, and stash it away under his desk. The manoeuvre is slick, but I catch it from the corner of my eye as I sit in one of the leather upholstered chairs.

"So, what then can I do for you today, daughter?"

"I seem to have stumbled across a... um... situation that I hope you can help me with."

His normally stormy grey eyes morph into near-stillness. "Of course, I'll do my best to oblige." He smiles and strokes his beard.

"I was hoping you might be able to break a curse?"

His hand drops to the table with a thud, and his eyes pierce mine. "Are you in trouble?"

"No, nothing like that father. I have stumbled upon Crocus—"

The storm reappears in his eyes, wild and blustering. "Where?"

"In the woodlands near my palace," I say in a muted tone.

"Here! On Mount Olympus?" he roars.

I cringe at the deafening volume, and I realise too late that I have divulged the centuries kept secret. And I dare not tell a mistruth "Yes."

*I hope the Fates forgive me.*

Zeus stands and starts pacing behind his desk. "Siriarna, this is an encumbrance I do not wish you to bear. I will have no more speak of curse-breaking."

"But the curse is unjust. I want to help him. I need to."

"Discussion closed, Siriarna. I will not have you subjected to the throes of danger. You are a newly anointed goddess, and you are susceptible to corruption. I won't allow it. The Furies cursed Crocus for his deceit, and I will not question their judgement, nor their punishment." His tone is firm and rigid. He sinks heavily into his chair, and folds his arms across his rapidly pulsating chest. There will be no bending of my father's will today.

The failure of my personal mission in helping Crocus engulfs me like an ominous shadow, and I look to the window to shed some light. Movement startles my vision. And I squint until I see the elongated wingspan of a vulture, hovering in line with the den. Its fixated red eyes meet mine, and send today's second chill down my spine. Only this time, the hairs on the back of my neck remain raised.

Zeus draws my attention from the window. "I'm only doing what is best for you, child. You must abide." His tone is dismissive, and his eye contact ceases.

"I understand. Thank you father... for clarity."

As I leave the den, I pass Bia. She smiles, but doesn't stop to speak. Instead, she enters the den.

A quick scan of the hallways reveals I am alone. Retracing my steps, I press my ear to the closed timber. "Keep an eye on her Bia," Zeus says. There are—"

"What are you doing?"

My neck swivels so quickly, like a flash of lightning, and I come face to face with Hermes. "I'm just leaving." I say promptly, my face flushing red.

"Perhaps I will tell Zeus you are lurking in the shadows," he says, smirking.

He hasn't forgiven me for Alexandraya's quick departure, and I honestly don't blame him. "Do what you will."

******

By the time I exit the palace, there is no sign of the vulture. Just a cheery cerulean horizon, dotted with a smattering of white puffy clouds. Perfect weather for a lengthy stroll home now that Bia is otherwise occupied with Zeus.

When I reach the woodlands, my heart drops. My feet trudge through the trees, and over the sprightly undergrowth that has popped up overnight. But I roam absent-mindedly until I reach the hollow.

"Siriarna, it's good to hear you again," the Crocus flowers echo.

"I'm afraid I've not come bearing good news." I say, shuddering a deep sigh. "I have been unsuccessful in finding a way to break your curse. And my father refuses to intervene. In fact, he has forbidden me from helping you," I whisper.

The flowers droop in mass movement, and my bruised soul weeps.

"I make my own decisions, Crocus. I am, after all, Goddess of Above, and I believe releasing you is my immortal-born duty."

"The last thing I want is for you to betray the King of Gods, Siriarna. Perhaps you should refrain from visiting."

"I won't give up, Crocus. And I won't be chained, not by anyone, not even my father."

Out of nowhere, southern winds gale through the

hollow forming a vicious whirlwind as they trap within the circular tree walls, stalling any further conversation.

Celeris zooms into the hollow and positions himself in front of me, his frame providing a shield from the gusty weather. But the fierce tracking wind manages to whip through the gaps, and I find it hard to stay upright, despite my divinity.

Crocus' voice cuts through the bluster, "You need to leave now Siriarna. I fear these winds will only escalate. Destiny is fickle, and I fear she has been twisted."

Celeris folds onto his knees and I swing my legs over his back. The Crocus flowers sway in a turbulent goodbye as the equine spreads his legendary wings and speeds out of the hollow. As we glide to the skies, I glance down at the secret resting place of the mortal-turned-flower, and notice a faint haze of red churning above the sanctuary.

The airstream has calmed when Celeris lands in the woodland at the edge of my palace. "Stay safe, my friend. And watch over Crocus. I will not stop searching for answers," I whisper, farewelling the horse with a scratch behind his ears.

Hooves stamp their approval, and Celeris is air bound in one swift beat of wings.

Striding to the palace door, I thrust open the entry doors, and climb the stairs two at a time until I reach the top floor. Here, I leap over the pile of books at the base, hurdling myself to the middle of the bed, where I cross my legs and sequence the day's events in my mind. Rubbing my temples from the relentless replays, my head a jumble of happenings, the puzzle finally unravels: Hera's blood red cape; the piercing red eyes of the vulture; and the haze of red circling Crocus and his hollow.

*The Furies.*

My stomach knots at the realisation, and I take this moment to pray to the Fates, "Please give me strength."

My wishes are answered when a shimmer of pure white light fills my room. Three entities appear before me, standing together in unison. They glow in ethereal translucence hovering between a spiritual and corporeal form. And they are more glorious than I had so-many-times imagined.

Taken aback, my voice eludes me, and all I can do is stare at the higher powers in front of me—a vision I never expected to encounter in person.

Details of my history and parentage resurface, and along with it, Eileithyia's punishment for divulging forbidden information. I sway backward, dizzy, and my eyes narrow at the unfairness the goddess who changed my life is suffering in her sealed cave palace.

The Fates answer my unspoken thoughts in a mellifluous tone, "A war is coming, Siriarna. We have no time nor desire to discuss Eileithyia, though she would agree that your safety is of the utmost importance."

They're right, Eileithyia has always put my wellbeing first. But I can't help the pain that winds around my heart at her incarceration, and red dances before my eyes.

"Do not give in to anger, Siriarna. The Furies have you in their sights. The veil is lifting—a shift has pierced its gleam—and with it their intentions," their voices chorus in harmonic synergy.

"Whatever could they want with me? I have no score to settle." Although as I say the words, an image of Hera wearing a red cape materialises at the forefront of my mind.

"Until we know for certain, this spell will protect you so that Fury may not touch you," they chime. "Goddess of Above, we stand to protect you."

Three hands outreach, and the gentle thread of their protection weaves around my body like a breath of warm sunshine, marking it with a curlicue pattern, which soon fades to nothing. Their departing words haunt me, "Be strong, Siriarna. You will be tested to your limits. You must stay vigilant."

\*\*\*\*\*\*

A mere moment later, my body convulses. The pain is blinding. Literally. My sight has been replaced with a wall of white and my head pounds in excruciating agony. Violently, I drop to my knees and cradle my head. Then the memories come thick and forceful, clawing their way into my mind, released from their imprisonment.

Once returned to where they rightfully belong, the physical pain eases, but my heart is in pure turmoil.

*Braxton! Oh my gods...*

# CHAPTER 17

## Alexandraya

Time to farewell the Home Realm!

Ares has been true to his word and visits regularly when the moon is at its fullest. But tonight, I won't be waiting in the grasslands. Instead, it's time to initiate the last trial—the Trial of the Chase—Julienne's favourite trial. And truth be told, it's mine too.

Excitement bubbles as I change into my yellow Propensity training uniform. It's been a long time since the material hugged my skin, and it fits like the glove it was intended to be.

Casting a rainbow light spell to dance through my room as I pack my belongings, cheers me into a magically spirited frame of mind. And I hum as I prepare for the trial. It's the one that will win me my divine prize—Goddess Alexandraya.

Lugging the overstuffed travel bag downstairs ready to meet the chariot Mattias arranged, I set off to find Julienne.

She's in the kitchen garden sipping her early morning rose petal tea, reading a letter with knitted brows. A ping sounds as her clench on the tea mug cracks the delicate ceramic.

"Everything okay?"

She whips the letter into her pocket and mops up the spilt tea, then responds, "Fine. Are you leaving now?"

"Yes. The chariot is imminent."

Julienne stands and reaches out her arms as if she's going to hug me. And I stiffen. Julienne does not hug.

Instead of the embrace I thought was forthcoming, she swivels my body around and inspects my Propensity uniform, "Yes, this is quite bewitching. The colour suits you well. However, your hair does not shine like it has been brushed 100 times," she says frowning.

"I may have missed a few strokes," I sigh.

"Do not make a habit of that, Alexandraya. You are so close to the prize. You must keep up appearances. Played right, you will be drinking ambrosia by the year end. Power is the true gift," she reminds me.

My focus is steel-like and fierce. And if my calculations are correct, Ares will be hunting me down soon enough. A tingle swirls in my stomach, and a smile as bright as my Propensity uniform appears across my face. "Of course you're right, Julienne, thank you," I say kissing her on the cheek and pivoting toward the front door.

Mattias is waiting when I get there. "Farewell, my girl," he says steering me out the door, "I'll grab your bag."

Returning in mere seconds, he hoists me, and then my travel bag, into the chariot then raises his hand into a hurried wave. It's the strangest thing.

The chariot departs and cool air whips against my cheeks as we rise. All thoughts of the Home Realm are lost as my focus lasers onto the next stage of my journey— Evolirium.

\*\*\*\*\*\*

The lightly fragrant air and perfectly balanced afternoon temperature greets me as the chariot lands in Evolirium. And to sweeten my arrival further, both Melodie and

Davina are waiting at the edge of the Zen.

They rush forward and bale me into a group hug. The TON reunited. Roman let that nickname slip in one of our more intimate encounters. The memories heat my cheeks deliciously. I hope to relive some of them while I wait for Ares.

*After all, love is a myth, and power is the true gift.*

"Oh my Gods, you look amazing," Melodie says as soon as we are free from our tangled embrace.

"She's right Alexandraya, you do," Davina agrees.

"Thank you friends. It's great to be back, although it will only be for a short time."

"Is your new wedding date to Hermes set?" Davina asks.

The words catch in my throat for a split second before I grin and reply, "Actually girls, there's been a change of plan."

Synchronised is their gasp, and I laugh. "I can't wait to debrief, but tonight I must rest. Let's schedule it for tomorrow night."

They nod their heads, link their arms through mine, and we walk the pathway to our adjacent huts together. A formidable trio... a Trio of Nightmares.

Inside my hut, I walk straight to the wardrobe and throw open the doors. Shoving the array of hanging clothing aside, and using my foot to sweep the shoes sideways, I step into the space, and close the door as I sink into the tight, blackened space. Instantly, my shoulders relax. After an hour meditating, I'm entirely focused.

Humming, I slither into my favourite black satin slip, and pile my hair on top of my head, leaving a few strands loosely falling around my face. In the living area, I cast a spell that bathes the hut in an ambient orange glow. And then cast another to transform the furniture colour into a deep scarlet red as a tribute to Smilax, and as a visual reminder of what's at stake. With tingles thrumming through my veins, I shimmy myself into the wingback chair... and wait.

The knock at my door is neither gentle nor unexpected. In fact, it's not long after midnight. I had anticipated the arrival closer to dawn. He made quick work of finding me which sets my skin ablaze and my heart pounding. Game on. But I don't rise to answer. Not yet.

The banging becomes more insistent, and the hut shakes in response, but I hold strong and remain seated.

When I hear the exasperated huff of his breath, I open the hut door.

"Come in Ares."

"You're a difficult lady to find."

"And yet, you found me!"

# CHAPTER 18

## Braxton

The invitation flies under my door as dawn breaks on Evolirium. I've been awake for hours, pacing the hut, trying to adjust to my realm return. And more importantly, trying to reconcile the vow I made—and what exactly that means for Siriarna—and me.

With little interest, and as a distraction to my thoughts, I pick up the sleek black square that lies stagnant on the floor. As I turn the invitation over, the double-headed silver arrow emblem gleams monumentally. The Core. I knew the selection process was happening this year, but I thought I'd missed the cut. Closer inspection of the parchment reveals a faint outline of the cliff-face on the eastern side of the realm, along with a shadowed sun. The selection must be happening at twin phase when Apollo and Artemis eclipse their celestials, and Evolirium celebrates with a worship festival. The by-annual event is the perfect time for chosen students to slip away from the crowd unnoticed. Genius come to think of it.

Being a member of The Core was all I ever wanted. It's why I started trading nectar for tuition with the higher level students. That was, before Siriarna. And before I found the power to stop Nicholas. And while my initial motives are no longer a driving force, joining the elite group may be the very medium I need to affiliate with the Sky Realm and consort with the gods—specifically Siriarna. The timing couldn't be more perfect. Smiling, I dress in my red training uniform. And while I leave the hut yawning, I depart with a glimmer of hope.

"You look tired this morning," Sage says, joining me on the pathway outside my hut.

"Thanks for noticing."

"No problem." Then she nudges me in the arm, and says, "Actually, you always look tired," she says, raising her eyes.

She's not wrong. I've hardly slept since I made my oath to the Furies.

When we arrive at the Learning Centre, the Second Year hallway is already hectic with a mass of students intermingling before the day's lessons begin. My sightline finds Roman amongst a slew of semi gods, and I make a hasty entry into the Time Propensity classroom with Sage trailing behind. I have an immediate desire to speed time forward, and skip the day's training. But I remember my promise to High Power Omnisensus, and the upcoming trial, and sink into one of the red oval shaped chairs.

"Today, we will work on freezing Time," says Group Leader Gisella a moment later, a smile spreading across her face.

Scanning the room, I see my three peers sitting in their chairs, and Sage looking confused.

"Yes, Braxton and Sage... I Time froze you both while allowing Jakob, Claira, and Thomas to remain in the present. That's the focus of today's lesson."

Nicholas can attest to my proficiency with this spell, and I relive the moment my fist connected with his jaw. It brings a huge smile to my face.

Gisella mistakes the grin for enthusiasm for the high level spell, and before I know it, I'm the first to 'learn' the chant and put it into practice. While the other students falter, I thrive freezing each of my fellow semi gods one at a time.

"Well done, Braxton. You're a natural," Gisella says.

"Beginner's luck," Jakob grumbles under his breath.

*If only he knew how much nectar it took to perfect this particular spell.*

Hours and literal hours of Time manipulation leaves me with foggy thoughts, and a dizzy soul at the end of the training day. When we step outside the Learning Facility, the sun temporarily blinds my sight, further confusing my already jumbled mind. Stretching my neck by rolling my head around my shoulders eases some of the Time-caused tension.

"You look shorter," Sage says.

She really is perceptive. The weight of my vow has slumped my tallness, and sits heavy on my shoulders. "Perhaps your eyes are sitting lower after Jakob's disaster spellcasting."

She laughs at my joke. "No doubt."

As we leave the steps of the Facility, I pass the person I have no desire to see—Alexandraya. She gives me a crooked smile and says in passage, "Always great to see you, Braxton."

I'm left staring after her.

"Gods Braxton, I thought you were better than that," Sage huffs, and charges away leaving me standing alone on the steps.

# CHAPTER 19

## Alexandraya

Running into Braxton is never a good presage to my day. And today, his wilting frame and surly expression leaves an acrid taste in my mouth. Swallowing my distaste, I focus my attention on the task at hand—this morning's meeting with High Power Omnisensus.

He was informed of my arrival by Tyrone before I left the Home Realm, yet no welcome back parchment was pinned to my hut door as is customary. An unfamiliar flutter of nerves quivers in my stomach. And I know I will need to use every ounce of cleverness to convince the Authority to allow me to stay on Evolirium.

When he opens the door, his face is strained and he lets out a not-so-muffled sigh, before widening the door for my entrance.

As soon as I sit in the chair opposite his, I say, "I wanted to apologise for my previous rash exit, Sir."

His brow is furrowed when he responds, "It's just not the proper way to depart a realm, Alexandraya. You put me in a difficult position with the Sky Realm. When Zeus told me of his blessing for your wedding to Hermes, I had no idea what was going on, and it made me look foolish."

Nodding and focusing on his reddening face, I choose my strategy, "Sir, I did not intentionally plan for any of this." Then, I squeeze out a tear and let it splash on the desk in front and hitch my breath in rapid succession.

"Take a breath Alexandraya," he says clearly perplexed.

I swipe a pretend tear away with my fingertips, and slow my breathing. "It was all a game to Hermes. He pulled me into his world with promises and declarations, and I believed him. When he tired of the game, I was discarded. I thought he loved me," I wail, and expel more tears on demand—a trial perfected under Julienne's guide—which has served me well today.

*Although there is truth to these words, and my heart does beat rapidly at the mention of his name.*

High Power Omnisensus' eyes crease at the corners,

the pity clearly written across his face, "A terrible fate," he mumbles.

I know he's reminiscing to a time when Goddess Aphrodite was his lover. Some say she used her divine authority to ensure he fell in love with her—it gave her worship in all realms and fed her ego. Her eventual shun left him heartbroken. And that's the exact emotion I'm counting on today. "Can I please stay in the realm and return to my Propensity group? I'm a quick study and I'll catch up; I promise," I plead.

His answer is immediate, though his gaze is faraway, "I think that's the best course of action."

\*\*\*\*\*\*

I hold my head high as I enter the Second Year Light Propensity Classroom. And the chatter amongst students immediately ceases. Making an entrance has always been my specialty, and this one takes the crown—more to the point, returns it to its rightful place.

Scanning the all-white room, I notice the seat next to Roman is conveniently vacant. "Hi," I say with a bright smile.

I'm met with a silent stare. It's not what I had expected. Unlike the adoring gazes from the rest of the class, Roman's stare is indifferent.

Group Leader Xander enters the room, nods in my direction, takes his position at the front of the room, and waves his arms like a conductor.

Melodie casts a beam of rosy light around the room, and Davina follows her lead by casting a scarlet shade. The remainder of the class spell shades of oranges and reds, and the all-white room is now a kaleidoscope of woven light rays, dancing like a symphony performed by a powerful band. The crescendo being Roman's black light dramatically absorbing all surrounding light rays before evaporating. Thus, returning the room to its complete absence of colour.

When training ends and our class is dismissed, I lag behind until the room is mostly vacated, waiting at the door for Roman. When he approaches, I ask "I was hoping you might be interested in helping me catch up on my spells? Your display was quite magnificent."

His brows raise, "I'm sure both Melodie and Davina will be more than thrilled to assist you," he replies, leaving me staring after his lofty form as it saunters through the classroom exit.

His confidence oozes god-like arrogance. And I like it. A lot. I have to remind myself not to get caught up in the thrill of the chase, and concentrate on my goals.

*Oh, but he is tempting.*

The girls are waiting in the central Propensity hallway. "Let's go," I command, and they follow my accelerated Light speed lead from the Learning Facility.

The outside air whips against my face, slapping my mind into renewed focus.

We arrive swiftly at my hut and Davina gasps as she takes in the décor change. "Ah, very chic," she says, eyeballing the blood red couch and matching wingback chair.

"I felt like a change," I say shrugging.

"It's spicy. I love it," adds Melodie.

I take my seat in the wingback chair, stretch out my legs, and free my jet-black hair from its ponytail.

The girls sit on the couch opposite, Melodie lounges on the armrest. "So... fill us in," Davina says.

"Well, it all started with Siriarna—"

A knock at my door interrupts my story. Melodie springs from the armrest and opens the timber a fraction,

"Yes, she's here but she's not available now, Mykos. Perhaps try and catch her at break tomorrow," she says, slamming the door in his face.

"Continue," she says sweetly, returning to the armrest.

*Ah, my loyal maiden.*

My tone venomous, I spit, "The night of our Graduation Party, Siriarna cast me into The Void in an act of revenge."

Both Melodie and Davina's eyes are saucer-like. "Seriously?" they tune.

"But Hermes rescued me and flew me to Mount Olympus. Our wedding was set to go down in history."

The girls swoon but my mouth parches. Desperate to quench the dryness, I rush to my fridge, grab a mountain elixir, and take a huge gulp that wedges in my throat, refusing to budge. "The big shock is that it turns out Goddess Psyche is my long ago dead mortal mother's sister!"

"Oh my gods," Davina says. And a second later, she adds, "So you are a true descendent of royalty."

That makes me genuinely smile. My mortal genes are aristocratic—the tilt of my chin is automatic.

*I deserve immortality.*

"So how did Siriarna stop the wedding?" she asks.

My fingernails scratch my palm, but I stop before they draw blood. "Psyche walked me down the aisle. Everything was perfect. Then Siriarna, standing next to Roman—neither invited, and startlingly unexpected—opened her powers to the sky and had a meltdown."

"Her powers?"

"They take after her father," I say bitterly.

"Who is?" Melodie asks salaciously.

"Zeus."

"Siriarna is Zeus' daughter?" Davina says, her voice high pitched. "And Psyche is her mother?"

Whoosh... Melodie falls from the arm of the couch she is lounging on and crashes to the ground, most non-semi god-like.

"Surely, there's some mistake. She's too basic for divinity," Davina says her lips twitching.

"I wish it was a mistake."

*In fact, I wish she remained frozen by Time.*

******

A few hours after the girls return to their own huts, in the predawn remaining darkness, I slink out of my hut and wander the vacant dormitory pathways—I need a release.

Turning at the connecting junction, as I have done so many times previously, I sidle toward Roman's hut. But instead of walking to his door, my gaze drags to the hut opposite—Siriarna's. And I take a step closer. An eerie feeling creeps over my body and the hairs on my bare arms stand to attention. Then the scar on my leg begins to throb.

The physical trauma a reminder that grips my soul, and reinforces the lengths I must follow to claim my rightful place in the Sky Realm.

*We will meet again soon, cousin, next time on equal standing.*

# CHAPTER 20

## Roman

Though the hour is after midnight, I'm not sleeping. The movement outside my hut is slight, yet I catch it, past experience forewarning exactly what to expect— Alexandraya. Perhaps subconsciously, that's why I'm wide awake staring out my window.

After our last encounter at Hermes' palace, I thought our journey was forever condemned. But here she is, in smooth inky precision. And even though I want to ignore the depths of my feelings, my chest swells when I see her. A stark betrayal to my head, and a road that can surely only end in further heartbreak, I move to the door, ready to welcome her. But instead of moving to my hut, she turns to face Siriarna's former home, where she stands motionless. Then, she spins on her heel, and sprints down the pathway in the direction she came.

Without a second thought, I chase after her. When I reach the corner, my pursuit abruptly ends.

"What are you doing, creeping around the pathways?" Braxton says, stepping out from the shadows.

"I could ask you the same thing."

"Well, why don't you?"

The mutual dislike is electric.

"What are you doing roaming the realm during rest phase?" I ask, my voice brittle.

"I'm on my way to the Zen to practice my skills while everyone's sleeping. At this hour, the timeline won't affect the Propensity training day."

"Right, I'll let you get on with it," I say, roughly.

"You're wasting your time chasing after Alexandraya, Roman," he says with a curl shaping his lips.

His comment feels like a punch to the stomach. "What I chose to do with my time, and who I want to spend it with is none of your fucking business."

His bitter laughter echoes in the darkness.

I leave without another word.

The idea of meeting Alexandraya lost its appeal the

moment Braxton disrupted the impromptu rendezvous. My dislike for the guy has intensified threefold. I'm glad Siriarna is free from his grasp. And I savour that thought when I enter my hut.

On the entry floor, in the pitch darkness, beams a shiny silver shape. I immediately know what it is, and my pulse begins to thrum with excitement. The invitation to trial for a position within The Core. This is exactly the moment I've been waiting for. My chance to reunite with the Sky Realm—particularly Apollo, and Siriarna—and assist in vital missions to help humanity.

\*\*\*\*\*\*

There is a spring in my step when I enter the classroom this morning. The selection time and location for The Core trials was hidden in the black parchment of the invitation. I have exactly five days to polish my skills, and I'll need every spare second to prepare.

Alexandraya is perched in her seat, one leg crossed over the other, both resting daintily on my chair. "Good morning, Roman," she says. Her emerald eyes sparkle brightly, and her glossy lips turn up at the edges while her legs remain firmly in position.

"Hello, Alexandraya," I answer, shifting her legs to the floor as I ease into my chair.

She attempts to strike conversation, but instead of engaging, I swivel my chair to face away from her and chat to Kait instead. The hairs on the back of my neck quiver, tickled by her quick-tempered breath that wafts over my skin in warm feathery lashes. A familiar stir of desire rumbles in response, and I almost surrender and turn to face her. But the upcoming elite trial keeps me firmly in position.

Xander enters the classroom and takes his place at the front of the class. "Today, we focus on how to intensify the Light of day."

Although I hear Xander speaking, I'm not listening. And I'm definitely not retaining any information—my mind fixated on how to impress at the trials.

When a hand squeezes my shoulder, I'm startled back to reality. A quick scan of the classroom reveals I'm the only one left. And Alexandraya. "You were a million realms away. Anything I can help you with?" she offers.

"No, I'm good."

Her hand remains on my shoulder, and her gaze burns

into my eyes. I reach for her hand, and she flings it into mine, squeezing it tightly, and says, "I'm here if you need me, Roman."

While tempting, she is the one distraction I most definitely do *not* need.

# CHAPTER 21

## Braxton

No training takes place during the Eclipse Celebration Festival. All hands are utilised to ensure the worship is remarkable. A gift from the gods is a gift to heed.

This year's tribute has been crafted by the Earth Propensity—an overly large duplicate celestial tribute stands lofty in the centre of the Zeneym Arena. Moonflowers twine through the hollow woven circle of branches, waiting in situ for their chance to bloom.

With preparations complete, there is little time remaining to change into black mission uniforms, the darkened clothing playing homage to the eclipse. The atmosphere is thick with anticipation, and I feel a shove in my side during a mass exodus out of the arena. Ahead of me is Alexandraya, a smirk wicked across her face. I'm tempted to Time-brand her with that expression, so everyone can witness her *true* face. But I don't want to expose the depth of my magic before the trial.

In my hut, I dress quickly in the mission uniform I haven't worn since last year. Memories of Siriarna flood my mind. And all of a sudden, the weight of past feels heavier than the invisible load that rests on my shoulders. Our reunion is all I've thought about since I made my vow. And becoming a member of The Core is a sure-fire way to link our futures.

*I can't let anything stand in my way.*

Returning to the Zen without delay is my number one priority.

When I arrive, the arena is entirely ready for the event—a trestle of white oak tables runs down the far side near the river—rows of neatly placed vials containing clear liquid sit on top.

Moving through the Zen my vision darts around the arena, scouting for the ideal exit. During the search, I find Sage and Jakob sitting on the grassy mounds.

"Join us," Sage says.

My palms are slicked with sweat as the eclipse draws

nearer—a Time wielder's worst nightmare. "What's up," I say, wiping my hands across my thighs, hoping the easy banter will distract me.

"I was asking Sage why she thinks you're able to wield new spells so effortlessly," Jakob says.

*Perhaps not so easy.*

"I guess it's just a natural talent," I answer, and shrug.

"Really? My guess is that you've been trained by a higher level student. What I can't work out is why anyone would risk banishment?"

"You're mistaken, Jakob."

"I'm sure I'm not—"

Sage interrupts the interrogation, her face is tinged red, "I told you, you were way off mark, Jakob."

"And I told you that something doesn't add up, Sage," Jakob spits.

High Power Omnisensus rises on a floating dais that comes to a standstill in front of the centre tribute, saving me from a head-to-head with Jakob. After a moment, his voice booms through the Zen, "Welcome one and all. Today, we bear witness to the spectacular event that is the eclipse. When daylight becomes shadowed, we embrace our heritage and our purpose. Please take a vial and drink."

Jakob stands and storms away. Sage turns to me and says, "Don't worry about Jakob. He's extremely jealous of your skills."

"Thanks for having my back."

"No problem, Time wielder. Let's go get ourselves a vial!"

There is only one vial remaining on the oak table when we arrive. "You have it," Sage says.

"I insist you drink it," I answer with a grin.

She doesn't argue and swigs the drink in one gulp, then sticks her tongue in the vial lapping for remnants.

"That good?"

"Mm, you have no idea."

My muscles tense at the sudden appearance of Apollo shooting through the sky in his golden chariot which sends the crowd into a frenzy.

*It's almost time.*

Apollo brandishes a golden lasso and throws it around the sun. His horses gallop the chariot higher into the horizon until it idles mid-point over Evolirium.

Artemis makes her entrance almost immediately after her brother in a silver chariot, the moon luminescent, strung behind her by a rope of pearls.

Her appearance causes Sage to faint. Reaching down and helping her to her feet, I'm met not with a dazed expression, but with a grin as bright as the very moon Artemis commands. "I just adore her," she says with wide eyes.

"She is rather spectacular," I say. But I don't think Sage heard a word I said, her eyes hunting every movement the goddess makes.

It's my opportunity and the perfect time to escape.

As the eclipse occurs, the moonflowers woven through the tribute celestial spring to life, their sweet enchanting aroma filling the Zen.

Bellows of cheers rocket skyward when each student is surrounded by a halo of light in the darkness. The vials—they must have contained an Earthly Propensity spell. My relief at not ingesting the liquid is amplified by the sound of my heartbeat ringing in my ears. But oh what a show for the gods above. Apollo and Artemis acknowledge the efforts of the realm by zig zagging their chariots in a show of metallic magic—their arrows exploding on contact, showering the realm with bubbles of light.

Pocketing a bubble, I slip out of the Zen.

As the distance between the festival and myself lengthens, the daytime darkness intensifies. I reach the eastern cliff unaided, but the track down the rock face is sketchy, and I slip taking my first step. Extracting the stolen bubble, I use its glow to light my way.

"Thanks for the light," says a honeyed voice from behind me.

"Kind of clever, actually," says another.

Then a new voice echoes through the shadows, "Wait up. Need some more light?" says a voice I'm way too familiar with. Roman.

A vein throbs at my temple. He's the last person I want to work with. Although, there's still hope he doesn't make the cut.

Roman jogs to stand beside me, his Propensity light ball hovering in his hand. When he recognises me, a scowl creases his forehead. "I'll take it from here. My light source is bigger than yours!"

*Smug asshole.*

He steps ahead, and I have the sudden urge to shove him down the vertical track, but my future rests on this trial and I refrain, hard as it is.

When we reach solid ground at the bottom of the

track, a semi god dressed in an elite uniform appears from the shadows. "Welcome to The Core trials. My name is Brielle. You have been chosen to participate in the Trial of the Worthy. If you succeed, you will become a member of The Core. It's as simple as that," she says matter-of-factly.

Glancing around, I count nine contenders. All are from Year 6 with the exception of Roman and me.

"Form a straight line," Brielle orders.

The nine of us scatter into position quickly, her tone obliterating any misinterpretation.

Brielle paces before each of us slowly before returning to her position in front of the line. She points out the two semi gods with bodies lit by glowing halos, "Leave and never return," she says.

They try to protest, but she waves her hand and motions to the track. Then she turns to the remaining seven, and says, "We are an elite stealth group. Our very foundation is to act without being seen. We will not allow stupidity into the elite."

Another semi god laughs, and says, "What losers," under his breath.

Brielle stalks forward and glares at the culprit, "Go. We do not chastise our own."

"B-but—"

"I said get out of here," she screeches.

Six contenders remain.

"Now, the rest of you... hitch a ride on either Apollo or Artemis' chariots and return with one of their arrows."

Any chance that this was going to be a straight forward trial has now been squashed a thousand times over. I scan the faces of the remaining semi gods, one of whom I recognise as Charlie, my nectar-traded tutor—he doesn't seem to recognise me—or he's pretending he doesn't. Panic is plainly written across their faces, all but Roman's.

*Smug asshole.*

"Time is ticking," Brielle says, grinning.

A scramble of feet thud up the track. I swerve out of the way of an avalanche of loose stones, but the semi god behind me is not as quick.

*That leaves five.*

I'm the last to reach the top of the cliff face, and time is fast running out. I sprint to the Ovallium Forest, having hatched a plan during my climb. Leaning against a tree by the river, I snatch a moment to catch my breath.

"Hey, Braxton," Charlie says.

*So he did recognise me.*

"Where did you come from?" I say.

"I followed you. You really should check over your shoulder, bud."

Great, I've got the best Time wielder on Evolirium in direct competition. I picture Siriarna in my mind, and a steely determination settles my nerves.

A reflection in the river catches both Charlie's and my attention. He tries to shove me aside, but the mirror image shows two chariots, and he drops the wrestle. "You take Apollo," he says.

There's no chance in Fury I'm going to hitch a ride with Apollo, though stealing his arrow does appeal. "Nah, he's all yours, my sights are set on Artemis."

His brows arch but he nods and we spread a width apart. Apollo approaches first and Charlie launches himself into the chariot.

Artemis follows her twin, an arrow aimed at Charlie's back. I could let her fire before accosting her chariot, but I take a leap of faith and land before she releases her weapon. She turns to me, her face a clap of thunder, the arrow still in hand. "How interesting," she says. "Did you come to rescue your friend by offering yourself in sacrifice?"

"Actually, I was hoping you might give me a chance to outrun your arrow. I know how you love a good hunt."

Her reply is swift, "You have a deal semi god. I must commend your bravery. What is your name? Though I will most likely forget it."

With a glint in my eye, I answer, "Braxton. And my Propensity is Light, so it is unlikely you will catch me, even with your arrow poised."

Her laughter is as silvery as her chariot. And a drop of saliva spills from her lips. She has been called to the Hunt and the challenge beckons like a beacon. "Such a shame to extinguish such an assured ray of light."

The chariot lands and Artemis waits for me to exit. As I turn my back, I bring the Ribbons of Time to my palm, then step into the Ovallium Forest. The exhale of the Goddess is hot and gusty but instead of running, I turn and glare at her. When she realises I've played her, her mouth twists into a snarl, but I've already twisted the Evolirium chord and she is frozen in Time.

Carefully, I prize the arrow from her grip and pace through the Forest, clinging with all my might to the Time ribbon. When I reach the cliff face, I release the realm and a split second later, the eclipse is over. And so is any chance of working with the Goddess in the future. But the risk was worth it.

Roman, Charlie and Laci, who I now recognise in the daylight, are standing in the cave at the bottom of the cliff face when I arrive, also holding arrows.

Brielle moves in front of us. "Welcome to the Core," she says.

******

My elation evaporates the moment I return to the Zen and run into Alexandraya. "Why so perky?" she says.

"You wouldn't understand."

"Try me."

"Ah, thanks, but I think I'll pass. I'd say it's nice to see you, Alexandraya, but it never is. I'd much rather be alone." I say with mock sincerity.

Her smile widens, but it does not reach her eyes. She stares my chest like she sees the tattoo and its fiery addition, and says, "You're never really alone now, are you, Braxton?!"

# CHAPTER 22

## Roman

When Brielle unveiled the trial, I had to cover my mouth to hide my glee. Completing the task was as easy as a walk in the meadows. I simply waved Apollo down and asked him for an arrow—he happily obliged. The only surprise was watching Braxton return holding one of Artemis' silver arrows.

*He always seems to show up at the most unfortunate of times.*

I was certain he would fail the trial—he's definitely not worthy. His cagey nature has been amplified of late. I don't trust him.

And now, he's locked in conversation with Alexandraya. The discussion seems heated, and my vision blurs as my eyes crease to a squint. First Siriarna and now Alexandraya. I'm ready to storm the union, but a hand on my shoulder drags my attention away. It's High Power Omnisensus. "I need you to come with me, Roman," he says in all seriousness.

As I walk beside the authority, he doesn't offer any conversation, which is entirely out of character. The silence makes for an awkward journey.

When we reach his office, I sit opposite his desk, and ask, "What's going on, Sir?"

He scratches his chin stubble and says, "I'm sorry, Roman, your guide father has passed."

Tears prick my eyes, and I can't hold them back. Vincent was the kindest soul in the realm and even though I knew his age was progressing at 487, he seemed indestructible to me.

He used to say how blessed by the gods' he was when Goddess Eileithyia put me in his and Galena's care. Thinking of Galena makes my heart break a little more. Half Vincent's age, she was the light to his torch. "I have to return to the Home Realm," I say urgently.

"I have arranged a chariot for tomorrow, Roman. In the meantime, Galena sent this for you."

He hands me a small box—the one Vincent and I made together out of ancient oak when I was nine years old. He'd collected the wood centuries earlier and said he was saving it for when I was old enough to understand the art of crafting. Together we worked the wood into the square-shaped box. Vincent said it was to house my special things. "Thank you High Power Omnisensus," I say leaving his office.

"I'm very sorry, Roman."

I leave the Authority's office and use my Light speed to burn off my sorrow. Through the Zen I race, past the dock and into the Ovallium Forest where I sit at the edge of the treescape staring through the filtered light to the sky above, my mind wandering to my childhood. Reliving the memories eases some of the heartache.

When I finally return to my hut, I open the box Galena sent. Inside is my favourite toy car, currently sapphire blue. I used my powers to alter its exterior each week—blue was Vincent's favourite. He said it reminded him of Galena's eyes, and a deep sob wells in my throat at the memories invoked.

A knock at my door forces me to swallow my grief before I answer it. Standing in all her glory, is

Alexandraya. "What are you doing here?" I say, weary.

"I heard the news Roman, I'm so sorry," she says, charging into my small living space.

"I'd like to be alone."

Unabashedly, she steps forward, wraps her arms around my neck and gazes at me with wide, inviting eyes. "No one should be alone at a time like this."

I draw in a sharp breath, but don't pull away from her embrace, nor do I break eye contact.

Without a word, she coils her legs around mine and pulls herself up my body; then forcefully presses her lips to mine. My body answers automatically, and I bury my pain within her full, pouty mouth.

The kiss is rough and urgent, and Alexandraya matches every stroke of my ravenous tongue with hers. Crushing her body to my chest, her legs still wrapped around mine, I carry her to my bed where we fall breathlessly. She uses the strength in her superbly toned legs to pull me inside her, and I growl low and guttural into her mouth. Snaking my arm underneath her back, I swing her on top of me in one rugged movement. My hands grip her hips tightly, and I move her body up and down until sweat glistens her skin. She arches her back and grinds herself into me, crying out in pleasure. And I'm lost, my own release a satisfying reprieve—my misery temporarily forgotten.

******

When I wake at the emergence of the new day, my bed is cool. I am alone, and grateful to be. It's near time to meet the chariot and return to the Home Realm for Vincent's Passing Ceremony.

Before I leave, I grab the little oak box, and add Alexandraya's pendant to the keepsake. As I replace the lid, I notice a small carving on its underside—a bow and quiver of arrows. I run my fingers over the inlay and wonder when Vincent added this symbol. And why?

# CHAPTER 23

## Alexandraya

Stretching my arms above my head in delicious slowness, I replay the events of last night over in my mind. Roman's normal gentle character was frenzied with angst and severity. He unabashedly fulfilled his need, at the same time furnishing what I craved the moment I saw him in class.

*So much potential. Such a shame he was born a semi god.*

Slipping out while he slept was an easy escape and one I've routinely made countless times previously. And now that he's out of my system, I can concentrate on my end game.

A sense of calm cloaks my soul as I pour myself into my Propensity uniform. Everything is slotting perfectly into place. The only slight glitch is Braxton. He will be difficult to work with, though my persistence will eventually wear him down. And, he will soon realise, he has no choice.

Humming, I close the door behind me, and join Melodie and Davina who are waiting on the pathway in matching Propensity uniforms. Together we commence our routine stroll to the Learning Facility.

"You're awfully cheery this morning," Melodie says.

"I had an epiphany last night," I respond smirking.

"Is that what you're calling it now?" Davina laughs.

The light hearted jest is spoiled by the sight of Braxton in the meadows. His scowl in my direction is not unnoticed by the girls.

"What's his problem?" Davina asks.

"Our paths crossed in the Home Realm. It wasn't inspired."

Melodie sighs, "Such a waste. Although, he seems to have pulled himself together since returning. Less reckless."

"It's almost like he's waiting for something," Davina adds.

Her comment triggers a thought, and then it dawns on me. He's not waiting for something, he's waiting for someone... Siriarna. His vow and his sacrifice must have been for her.

*Why?*

The thought of my cousin causes my hands to ball into fists. Ever the thorn in my side. My mind whirs into action, I will not succumb to further sabotage. It's time to accelerate my plan. She will not best me twice.

Distracted, I almost run straight into Mykos, who's blocking the Learning Facility's entrance. "Hello Alexandraya," he says, sidling up beside me.

The collective groan from the girls mirrors my own sentiment, "Mykos, it's good to see you," I say brusquely, releasing my grip.

Undeterred, he says, "It's great you're back, we should hang out at the Etherial Room later."

"I've no time at the moment, I'm trying to catch up on my spells."

His face falls, but he persists, "Right, of course you do. When you're ready? Maybe, next week?"

"Maybe."

"Bye, Mykos," Davina says, linking her arm through mine and Melody's, dragging us through the Second Year veil, and into the refuge of our Propensity classroom.

Here, I take my seat next to Roman's now vacant desk.

My brows furrow, but I've no time to waste chasing the past when my future is hovering close enough to taste. That's the truest present, and the gift I crave with insatiable voracity.

My thoughts stagnate on the growing possibility that Braxton's vow relates to Siriarna and somehow involves her return to Evolirium—which would be catastrophic to my current plans. I can't let that happen. I have to protect my destiny. I have to speak to Braxton. Now.

Clearing my throat, I interrupt our Group Leader, "Excuse me Xander."

"Yes, Alexandraya, what is it?"

"I'm not feeling well. I need to return to my hut."

His muddy brown eyes scrutinise my face, but he relents, "Rest up, and we'll see you tomorrow."

His response is as expected, and I bite down on the inside of my cheek to stop the triumph from spreading across my face.

Gathering my satchel, I whisper instructions to the girls to meet me at my hut after lessons, then amble toward the exit.

Released from the constraints of the classroom,

outside in the open air, I suck in a breath of fresh air. The warmth of the sun's rays seeps into my skin and gently heats my blood—the hallowed kiss of the Progression Realm.

Serendipitously, I discover Braxton sitting alone in the middle of the meadows.

*Why is he always lurking in the meadows?*

"Braxton."

"What do you want, Alexandraya?" he replies.

"Yesterday, I may have been a bit snappish."

He raises his eyes.

"Look, I know we're not exactly friends—"

His laughter is low and brittle. "True, we are definitely not friends," he says coolly.

"Well, as a non-friend, I should warn you that forcing Siriarna's return to Evolirium will end in heartache and chaos. I'd hate your vow to have been for nothing."

His face turns a deep red, and he spits the words... "You know nothing of true love."

My teeth grind against each other. "True love has many faces, Braxton, and is not always defined in flesh."

"Stop playing games, Alexandraya. My vow has nothing to do with you."

His anger has given me the answer to my question—Siriarna is returning to Evolirium—and I must leave immediately. "Take care Braxton," I say, and use my Light speed to leave the meadow and Braxton behind.

In the confines of my hut, I reach my hand into my yellow training pants, pull out a bindweed berry, place it in my mouth, and swallow. Two remain.

"Hello, Alexandraya," Smilax's voice instantly fills my head.

I jump straight into conversation, "The full moon approaches and with it, Ares' arrival will follow."

"It's time to return to Mount Olympus," she says, her voice silky smooth.

"I will do my best to expedite my homecoming."

"It is almost time," she confirms.

"I am ready."

A blinding energy swamps my mind as a torrent of pent up centuries old emotion floods through my soul. So forceful is the sentiment that I begin to shudder, tripping on the rug beneath my feet as I stumble backward. A vine-shaped weave of light buoys my body upright before I crash to the floor. It is the first time our connection has manifested to physicality.

"Thank you Smilax," I breathe, but my connection with the bindweed has been severed.

While I am once again alone with my thoughts, my heart fills with a wisp of hope, and a promise of a future almost present.

# CHAPTER 24

## Alexandraya

The evening's anticipated full moon somewhat releases the tension that rests on my shoulders. Like an unwanted shadow lurking behind, Siriarna's arrival haunts my hours.

Tonight I will cement my return to the Sky Realm. In my mind's eye, I see the golden gates of Mount Olympus and my glorious return. My stomach whirs in excited anticipation—tonight, for better or worse, it will be done—the final phase of courtship before I fulfil my vow.

To pass time and take my mind off the importance of the rendezvous, I throw on a pair of plain black running shorts, a matching tank top, and slip on my favourite pair of running shoes. All set, I head out of my hut for one final voyage around Evolirium.

The hour is before daybreak, and I creep along the pathway, weaving my way through the dormitory huts in silence. Once I'm past the junction and on my way to the meadows, I cast a Light speed spell.

Heat spreads through my body as the energy flows through my veins, and my pace increases to a blur. Through the realm I zoom effortlessly, dashing past the Zeneym Arena to the Ovallium Forest and beyond until I reach my final destination at the top of the mountains.

Here, the temperature plummets and the icy breeze feels like frozen fingers caressing my bare skin. The peacefulness of being alone fuels my mind, and the little puffs of heated breath that spiral from my mouth remind me of Smilax's leafy tendrils.

A thrill shoots down my spine at what is forthcoming, and I shiver despite the temperature acclimatisation.

Watching in synchronisation as the last of the darkness peels away and the sun begins to breach the realm in hues of vibrant red, feels utterly symbolic—almost as if Apollo created the sunrise just for me—yet is unlikely given his allegiance to Siriarna.

My time in the mountains draws to a close when my

skin is tinged with blue, and my fingertips begin to numb. Before my descent, I take one last sweeping gaze around the snow-capped peaks, and the realm splayed out below. "Goodbye Evolirium," I holler into the vast and brightening horizon.

The declaration is finite and liberating.

Flexing my tingling fingers to cast my power, I race toward my hut, the Light speed thawing my chilled flesh. And while the dorms remain largely sleepy, I spy Braxton slinking into his hut, wearing the same clothing I saw him in yesterday afternoon. He's alone. Siriarna is nowhere in sight. And though I curse myself for my weakness, I breathe a sigh of relief.

Instead of returning to my hut, I head to Melodie's for a pep talk, knowing Davina will be right behind me. A TON support is what I crave.

Melodie's hut is a blast of music, and I push open the door to let myself in. She is totally oblivious to my arrival, belting out lyrics of the latest realm folk song in a voice that warrants her namesake. When she twirls during the chorus, she spots me, and says in a singsong voice, "Good morning, Alexandraya."

"It is indeed."

She appraises my running gear and says, "Early morning run? You must be in plotting mode."

"You know me too well." I laugh at her perception—she has witnessed this ritual many times over the years.

Charging into the hut with a tray of bubbles, exactly as I predicted, is Davina. "You guys started the party without me," she says, passing us each a glass.

"There's no party," Melodie says laughing. "But I think dawn drinks are definitely in order."

I rest the glass on my bottom lip, slowly tilt back my head, and swig a liberal mouthful of liquid. The spice of the elixir provides an instant dose of much welcomed valour. For tonight, I must convince the God of War to return me to the Sky Realm. Up until now, his interactions are reminiscent of a reigning battle strategy not dissimilar to how I would normally pursue my target. But this game of hearts is greater than a tussle of willpower. And winner takes all.

"Another?" Davina asks, gazing at my empty glass.

"For luck," Melodie chimes.

"For the love of gods!" I vow.

Melodie bursts into a poetic song of victory as Davina tops my glass. The tune is upbeat and buoys my frame of mind. As the tribute closes, she declares, "To the rise of Goddess Alexandraya."

"Cheers to that," Davina says.

****** 

With only a half day remaining till nightfall, and renewed self-confidence, I busy myself with preparations—perfection is the unified combination of genealogy and travail. And I've had many hours to refine my skills.

After an overlong shower, cleansing my hair and scrubbing my skin raw with rock salts; I rub meadow-honey balm into the fresh and pristine layer of exposed skin until it gleams. Then I dip my nails into a pot of scarlet polish, and allow them to drip dry in the temperate realm climate. The result is flawless.

Time has progressed quickly to sundown, and if I didn't already know of his punishment for past indiscretions, I'd assume Braxton manipulated the timeline.

Opening my wardrobe, I rummage through my clothing. Selecting an outfit is a painstaking process—it has to be just right. My fingers trail the simple black dress

I wore to the First Year Challenge winning dinner with the gods. And my heartbeat quickens when I remember the effect it had on Hermes. Oh how things have changed since then. Progressed in a way I could never have imagined, nor calculated. One moment I was destined to live a divine immortal existence in a beautiful palace with a garden of roses planted especially for me, and the next I was discarded like an expired bloom. The memory of an unexpected love story lost hiccups in my chest.

Reminding myself of the true gift, my focus returns, and I discard the dress along with its tangled past. Instead, I select a navy blue playsuit with sheer billowing sleeves, and fasten a red belt around my waist.

Picking up my brush from the side table, I slide it through my already air-dried silky, smooth hair knowing with a further hundred strokes the glossy black strands will gleam like a mirror under the night sky.

As midnight approaches, I'm ready to add the final and most important element before heading to the dock. Uncorking the little bottle of frankincense Julienne gave me, I trace the scent along my throat and add a dot to each wrist. The fragrance is breathtaking. I'm ready.

The breeze is gentle when I arrive, causing ripples of

waves to splash across the top of the river. Sitting at the end of the dock, dangling my legs over the edge, I peer into the water below, and smile at my shimmering reflection.

At precisely midnight, as expected, Ares arrives. He dips down beside me in fierce effortlessness, and I angle my face toward him allowing the moonlight to waltz across my skin.

"It's good to see you Alexandraya," he says in the stoical tone that fits his title, and for which I have become accustomed to.

"As it is you," I reply, slanting my body so the sheer material falls from my shoulder.

His obsidian eyes blaze with hunger as he breathes the frankincense that scents my skin. "We should make it a more frequent occurrence."

I trace my tongue over my lips, glistening them with moisture. "I'd like that. If only we didn't reside realms apart."

He strokes the side of my face with rough fingers, and asks, "Would you be open to returning to Mount Olympus?"

Instead of replying, I shift my gaze into the river, and twist a lock of hair around my finger.

Ares tilts my chin.

"How could I refuse such a generous offer?" I say, meeting his eyes and curling a hand into his.

His grip tightens around my palm, "We should leave at once," he says, his voice gruff.

"As you wish."

# CHAPTER 25

## Braxton

Watching the moonflowers and evening primrose blossom under the night time luminescence is sweet torture. It's the reminder of the perfect night lost, but it also holds the promise of what has now been restored.

Every night when the sun slips behind the realm, I return to the meadows and linger until dawn. Hopeful of her return—hopeful that she still feels the same way.

Tonight, however, it's the mane of jet-black hair swishing along the pathway that catches my attention. Alexandraya.

*Where is she going dressed like that at this hour?*

My first instinct is to follow her, but I will not risk the chance of missing a reunion with Siriarna. So I remain in the clover, staring at the flicker of blinking stars in an otherwise unblemished night sky. And hope tonight is the night the Fates take mercy.

When I see a chariot flash through the sky, Time stills, and not by my hand. A flood of yearning wraps its way around my being, and I am frozen in place.

*Could tonight be the one I've been waiting so desperately for?*

A wave of desire swirls in my stomach as I stare optimistically above. However, closer inspection reveals a familiar gleam of red. Two passengers ride the night, one a mighty god and the other a semi god with jet black hair streaming behind her. A guttural howl escapes my throat, but the only sound that rings through my ears, is the buzz of disappointment.

It's the unexpected gust of wind slapping against my face that draws my attention to the far edge of the meadow. Narrowing my eyes into focus, I spy a horse with beating wings and my jaw drops—where did it come from? These creatures are extinct.

It takes a few moments for me to register the goddess sitting atop the magnificent fabled animal. And when I do, I am awestruck—Siriarna, radiant in a halo of divinity.

She is everything I remember, and more than I could imagine. Dismounting in one smooth movement, she stands before me from afar.

My legs move before my mind catches up, projecting me toward the moment I have been dreaming would one day become reality. Though each step feels laden with led, I do not project time forward. I want to savour every second. Likewise, I do not swipe the tears that are pooling, a pouring of hard fought surrender.

As her face becomes nearer, my pulse races in glorious recognition. When I do finally stand before her, she drops to her knees, "Braxton, I... remember," she sobs.

Her words almost break me. I have longed for this moment. "You have no idea how desperately I've missed you, Siriarna. I wasn't sure you would ever return... to me," I say, swallowing the lump in my throat.

"I couldn't get back quick enough... to you," she says, her tanned skin flushing as pink as the primrose flowers surrounding us.

There are no words that can express how I feel right now, and I reach to hold her in my arms at long last.

At this motion, the horse beside her rears on its hind legs, and furiously flaps its wings before I touch her.

"Celeris, steady boy," she says.

But the horse's enormous smoky eyes lock onto mine and it releases a high pitched squeal that pierces an otherwise silent night.

I have little choice but to freeze Time around us, squeezing Evolirium's Time ribbon between my left thumb and index finger. Celeris, as she called him, is frozen mid frenzy.

"I don't know what's gotten into him. He's very protective, but there's nothing to worry about here," she says, glancing around the meadows.

"Siriarna, there's something I must tell you—"

"I won't let anything stand in our way, I have been robbed of too much time already," she says halting my confession.

Pulling her into a long awaited embrace, I cup her face with my right hand, and brush my lips across hers. As soon as our skin touches, my chest ignites in fiery agony, and I am thrown backward.

Siriarna simultaneously falls to her hands, and I watch a curlicue pattern appear across her skin in bright white. Her gaze settles on my torso and her mouth opens, but then she clamps it shut.

Following her stare, I level my sight where my scythe tattoo has scorched my shirt and is blazing red, "I can explain," I attempt feebly. Although, I'm not sure what's happening myself.

"Oh Braxton, what have you done?"

"I made a vow to return your memories," I blurt, and hang my head.

She cries into the night. And I fear the sound will haunt me forever. "We cannot be," she says.

"Please don't say that. I will do anything for you, Siriarna. There is no sacrifice I won't make. I love you."

Her face is ashen, "I love you too Braxton, but I cannot be touched by Fury. The Fates have made it so."

*Oh dear gods, no.*

My grip on Time slackens and Celeris swoops between us. Using his wings like arms, he lifts Siriarna onto his back and takes flight. Her body is hunched over, her shoulders jerking savagely, and her tears fill the meadow below in a torrential downpour of despair.

I can't lose her again, I can't. The Ribbons of Time appear in my palm and I twist to reverse what has just transpired. I need to see her again, to hear her say she loves me.

But instead of the timeframe adjusting, three figures descend, caped in red. The Furies. "We will not let you change what is set in motion," they echo.

My jaw clenches and I spit the words, "I will not bow down, and I will not lose her again."

Their laugh is hollow as it wraps itself around my body like a straitjacket. "You have no choice semi god. It will not be undone. And in Time soon, we will collect your vow."

They wave their arms and I am kneeling before them, completely at their mercy. My chest burns at their whim and my soul reaps no joy.

I see a combined smirk through the haze as the Furies disappear in a plume of red smoke.

My tattoo returns to its normal shade, but the scorching ache in my chest remains. While I may still have a part to play in whatever game Fury is playing, Nicholas has taught me a queen does not always hold all the power. And in this game of chess, I will not be the pawn.

# CHAPTER 26

## Siriarna

My head bobs back and forth upon my shoulders in time with my shudders, and I haven't the strength nor the will to hold it upright.

In a cruel twist of Fate, the mark on my skin fades the further I travel from Braxton. The red outline of his scythe tattoo is burned into my mind, along with the horror of its consequence.

As Celeris enters the vortex, angst flows in waves when I realise I'll be returning to my palace alone. The thought sits uneasy, and I whisper to Celeris to take me to Apollo, because the idea of being alone is too much to bear. And truth be told, I fear I will drown in my sorrow with a real possibility of flooding the entire Sky Realm.

It's after dawn when Celeris lands behind the stables, and I dismount onto shaky legs, "Thank you for your protection, my dear friend, I'll be fine now. Go before the realm awakens," I whisper to the horse.

He nudges his head under my hand, and I scratch his neck before turning to Apollo's door. As I raise my hand to knock, the door swings open, "Siriarna, to what do I deserve this visit—"

He stops mid-sentence when he sees my blank face, and I collapse into his arms. Shouldering my weight, he escorts me to his living room and eases me onto a chair, scrutinising my arms as he does so.

"Things could not be worse, I don't know what to do," I say miserably. The crevice in my heart widening with each repeat memory of the scene in the meadows.

Apollo picks up my arm closest to his body and runs his hands over the faded curlicue. The marks tingle at his touch. His eyes glaze over as he connects with the symbols. "Things have taken a turn the Fates did not expect," he says releasing my arms.

"Can they be remedied?"

His voice is crisp, "Your *friend* has committed a grave misconduct," he says shaking his head. "The consequences will impact us all."

"He was only returning what was rightfully mine. He did not weigh up the cost. And in all honesty Apollo, I'm glad for their return," I say defiantly.

His face does not soften. "Some things are best left forgotten."

My face turns as red as a Sky Realm sunset when I realise he has witnessed the night I spent with Braxton in the meadows. "Not this."

"Siriarna, there is a better match for you should you open your eyes, and your mind. You are immortal and have an eternity to feel the way you have previously. Maybe better."

*How utterly mortifying.*

"Thank you for your hospitality, Apollo. I think it's best I leave—"

I don't wait for his response. Instead, I stalk from his palace door straight into the stable, where I jump in his chariot and command Acteon and Lampos to return me to my palace. The horses comply with a shake of their manes, and gallop across the realm as instructed.

The only positive outcome from the humiliating interlude is that the misery I bore when arriving at

Apollo's palace, has been replaced with sheer and utter exasperation.

"Thank you," I say to the horses as their hooves trample the grass outside my door. "Your master is impossible you know."

Their whinny sounds like laughter and breaks my solitude. What I need is a hot scented bath to wash the dreadfulness of my current situation away—even if only momentarily.

Leaving Apollo's trusty steeds to frolic amongst the wildflowers that have sprung up on my lawn—I have suspicions that the nymphai had something to do with their sudden appearance—I dash to my bathing chamber.

When the water is near the brim, I step into the stone bath and duck my head beneath the surface. The lavender infusion doesn't bring stillness, nor calm to my mind. Only chaos occupies the space, taunting me with far away thoughts of Braxton. Images of our past, from memories newly returned, fill my head, and I grapple with the knowledge that we cannot unite. That a curse has stolen my destiny. And Braxton is my future. I feel it with every fibre of my being.

Leaving the bathing chamber wrapped in a towel, I

move carefully across the marble floor to my bedroom. From my wardrobe, I select a long-sleeved ankle length lilac chiton to cover the symbols that have remained faintly visible on my skin. I loosely braid my dampened hair and leave it falling over one shoulder. Then dart from the palace to Apollo's waiting horses.

And he's there, standing amongst my wildflower front lawn, scowl creasing his forehead.

"Where do you think you're going?" Apollo chastises.

"If you must know, I'm returning to Evolirium. I have unfinished business to take care of," I say.

Avoiding his glare, I pluck a handful of pale yellow flowers from the ground, and tuck them into my braid.

"That is unwise, Siriarna. Trouble is brewing. You witnessed that firsthand."

While my head agrees with the God of Sun and Light, my heart is begging for a reunion with Braxton. Even if touch is temporarily off the table, I have to believe there is a way to break the curse. I won't consider the possibility of permanence. "Okay, Apollo. I'll stay."

"I hope you do," he says, stepping into his chariot.

"I was just about to return it to you," I reply sheepishly.

"No harm done, I must fly. Be sensible, Siriarna," he says before leaving.

*Hmm, he seems distracted. Where is he off to in such a rush?*

At least he doesn't lag behind, because I'm about to break my agreement. Braxton is all I can focus on. But before I travel through realms, I need to speak with Crocus.

Ensuring the skies are free from Apollo, I amble to the forest, and wade through the thicket until I arrive at the hollow. The Crocus flowers greet me by swaying in the breeze, and I sit alongside the brook. "Hello Crocus."

"It's great to have you here, Siriarna," they chirrup.

"Where's Celeris?" I ask, noticing the absence of the winged horse.

"He's scouting the area, there has been an uptake in the winds of late. The Furies are not sitting idle—something is looming. And I fear it is not going to be pleasant."

The muscles in my body tense, and my foot slips from the rock it rests on. Dust scatters as I adjust my posture.

"Is everything okay, Siriarna?" the flowers question.

Biting my lip as Apollo's warning sinks in, I respond with new empathy, "My beloved has been marked by

Fury."

A drop of moisture drips from the throat of the flowers. Tears for a mortal life long ago forfeited. "The Furies are bound by vengeance. They punish those they deem wicked. Do you know of the crime for which he was accused?"

My face turns crimson, "He made a vow to return my memories."

"Then he will bear the weight of debt upon his shoulders until collected. You should not be affected by this obligation."

"That's just it, Crocus, I have been shrouded in protection by the Fates."

The flowers begin to sway wildly in a dance of foreboding, "A war is coming, Siriarna."

*I must warn Braxton.*

# CHAPTER 27

## Roman

Entering the Home Realm and knowing Vincent won't be waiting to greet me brings a knot of guilt to my stomach. I skipped the last chance to visit because I was in the Sky Realm with Apollo. So blinded by my favourite god's abilities, I selfishly missed the last chance of seeing my guide father alive.

It's Galena who's waiting for me now. Her normally long wavy hair has been cropped short, and her eyes are devoid of their normal sparkle. She puts on a brave face as she greets me, "Roman, it's good to see you."

I circle my arms around her frame and feel her skeleton beneath the long tunic she's wearing. "It's good to be home."

Together we walk to the tram station in silence. It's clear I must look after my guide mother and ensure she's eating properly, or I may be at risk of losing her too.

On the tram, I take off my pullover and wrap it around Galena's shoulders. She's shaking under the chill of the realm, but her eyes are trained forward—I doubt she even realises she's cold.

When we arrive home on the far western side of the realm, I am shocked to see the state she's been living in. The house is dark and musty, and all windows are closed with the blinds drawn. It resembles an oversized corporeal tomb.

Sensing my appraisal, she says, "I should have cleaned up a bit before your arrival. I'm sorry, Roman."

She looks so fragile, more so than I had imagined. "How about you pop into the living room and I'll make us a fresh cup of dandelion tea," I say in good spirits.

She nods and escapes into the middle room.

In the kitchen, I rummage through the crockery until I find a ceramic mug and saucer. I add a few biscuits, from an unloved packet sitting lonesome on the cupboard shelf, and take the refreshments to my guide mother.

She accepts gratefully and pops a biscuit into her

mouth. "I guess we should talk about the Passing Ceremony and make arrangements."

"No need to worry about that now. Let's get ourselves a good night's rest and start fresh tomorrow?"

Galena offers a perfunctory nod, and I take the opportunity to offer her another biscuit. She nibbles absently, and a rush of relief floods through me. While only minimal, at least she's consuming a little sustenance.

"How about we start that rest?" I say when the plate is empty.

"That sounds good, Roman."

Standing, I offer my arm. Galena wrenches herself from the armchair, and clings to it like a crutch. When she's steady, I lead the way. Arm in arm, we march down the hallway.

Her body stiffens when I open her bedroom door, and she takes two steps backward. "I haven't been in that room, since..."

Closing the door quickly, I manoeuvre Galena to the guest suite at the rear of the house. It appears to be where she has been sleeping. The bed is crumpled and unmade, but the side table holds a book and her reading glasses. "Good night Galena, I'll see you in the morning."

Bypassing my own room, I return to the living room and clear away the earthenware. Then, I open all the blinds and windows. Come morning, the house should be fresher.

It's not until the late evening hours that I return to my bedroom, and unpack my travel bag. Opening my bedside table to place my oak box, I find an envelope with my name scribbled in Vincent's handwriting. Picking it up and staring for too long, I brave the task and tear it open, revealing the letter inside.

My Dearest Roman,

I am so very proud of the semi god you have become. Watching you grow up has been my life's honour. Of which is coming to an end. I'm sorry dear boy, but my time in this realm is imminent. I ask you to help Galena in the weeks post my passing. She is going to struggle, my dearest sapphire always. Help her find her light Roman, for it is only you that can. Know I love you and know you have made me so proud. When you look to the stars above, it is me twinkling down upon both you and Galena, the loves of my life now and through eternity.

With all the happiness in my soul,

Vincent.

The last lines blur. *Oh Vincent, I could not miss you more.* Taking care not to tear the moistened paper, I fold it in quarters and place it in the oak box alongside Alexandraya's emerald necklace.

Although my body is plagued with exhaustion, I don't hold much hope that I'll rest this evening. So when I wake to an already risen sun, I'm dazed and a little disorientated.

In the living room, I find Galena sipping tea. "Good morning. Did you sleep well?" she asks.

She looks slightly brighter this morning, her cheeks less grey, and her eyes less sunken. "I did, thank you," I reply honestly.

"We should organise Vincent's Ceremony today, it's set to take place in five days." At her mention of the Passing Ceremony, Galena's shoulders droop along with her head.

"You know, I think we should celebrate the life of a

great man who I'm certain will be watching down on us from the clutches of the night sky, like the star he will become."

"Oh Roman, that is exactly something Vincent would say," she says jumping up and throwing her arms around me tightly.

"Let's do something crazy!"

Galena raises her eyes.

Casting a spell, I transform the buttercup yellow walls into a light pastel blue and change the white ceiling to an inky black.

Galena gasps at the shadowy change.

"I'm not finished yet," I say laughing. And I chant a spell that appears tiny twinkling stars scattered across the ceiling.

"Oh Roman, it's breathtaking," she says, tears pooling in her eyes.

"No more crying, Galena. We are going to celebrate the greatest man we had the honour of knowing personally. Let's plan the best send-off imaginable."

She nods fervently. And so we begin.

******

Today is Vincent's Passing Ceremony. Galena is dressed in a black tunic with long lace sleeves, her hair finished with a crown of daisies—Vincent's favourite. She looks youthful in her mourning, and I thank Vincent's letter, safely tucked into my trouser pocket, for helping me break through her grief.

Together we arrive at Imperial Lake to a gathering of people along the bank, waiting to send Vincent to the stars.

On a platform stands the Realm Leader, ready to officiate the Ceremony. Galena and I join him on the structure and Tyrone begins... "Thank you all for joining us today at the Passing Ceremony of Vincent. Vincent, today we commit your soul to the stars. May your new form carry you through a glittering eternity."

Galena's voice echoes around the lake in a hauntingly beautiful hymn of farewell. So beautiful is the rendition, I struggle to remain composed.

Bearers launch Vincent's hessian swathed body into the lake followed by a string of daisies that spread like floral wings. Floating candles flicker alongside the former life of Vincent and when the light reaches the hessian, the material ignites. Flames of amber rise as they engulf Vincent's body, claiming the last of his mortality. Using my Light Propensity, I cast a spell to change the burning warmth to a cool blue that changes to a brilliant sapphire the higher the flames climb.

Applause from the crowd erupts and I glance to Galena. She looks at me and smiles through silent tears. In this moment, I know I've sent Vincent off in a way that Galena will remember for the rest of her life.

Watching the last of the sapphire embers arch their way to the sky above, I notice a lone figure standing on the far embankment. From the stature, it looks to be a god and I wonder why in the realm a god would attend Vincent's Passing Ceremony.

My curiosity is interrupted by Galena clasping my arm. Together we descend the platform and walk through the crowd that has formed a semi-circle on either side of the lake's edge. A broken circle of life speared by the loved ones left behind. As we walk, we gesture to the skies above for the safe reincarnation of Vincent's soul to be laid in an eternal, peaceful rest.

Both Galena and I continue the Walk of Transient Souls all the way home, neither of us wanting to break the moment.

Aching for a reprieve from today's happy but emotional send-off, I launch from the doorway and flop onto the bed.

Reaching into my drawer for the oak box to replace Vincent's letter, my sightline lingers on the lid's engraving when I pop open the lid.

"Galena?" I say meeting her in the living room with the box.

"Yes, love," she answers.

"Do you know what this carving means?" I ask, handing her the lid of the box.

She runs her eyes over the carving, tracing her fingers along the detail. Then answers, "Vincent asked me to make sure you received this box after his passing. He said it held the truth."

My head spins in a frenzy of realisation. The figure on the embankment, and the invite to his palace after Evolirium's near destruction. Surely it cannot be?

*Apollo is my birth god.*

# CHAPTER 28

## Alexandraya

The wind whips through my hair as the chariot exits the vortex, and I hold my head high. The unruly strands conceal the smile that automatically lights my face the moment we enter the Sky Realm. Everything is slotting perfectly into its well-executed place. A small flicker of victory churns through my stomach, and raises my spirits.

Sneaking a peek at Ares, I notice his hands clutch the reins tightly, his posture rigid, and his jaw is set firm as he eases the chariot through the golden gates. He is every bit the epitome of the God of War.

His palace is located due north on top of the realm's highest peak. Like the god himself, the exterior is dark and foreboding, blending perfectly with the twilight hour.

Though the view is thwarted by evening shadows, the 360 degree vantage point is distinctly visible.

In the opposite direction, due south, is Hermes' palace. My sight lingers there for a second before the horses draw up at the palace entrance.

Ares lowers the ladder and steps from the chariot, steadying the rungs before I descend. "Welcome home."

"Thank you for bringing me back," I say as my feet meld into the earth.

"Let me show you around," he says leading the way through the solid oak front door, flicking on the lighting as he enters.

Following behind, I keenly observe the collection of spears, armour, and shields mounted to the entry hall as I pass. In the lounge room hangs a plethora of frescos depicting boars, dogs, wolves, and vultures. Every wall is covered. It's intense and masculine, and could definitely use a woman's touch. "It's very... rugged."

"I knew you would appreciate it."

Up the solid spiral stairway I trail. The landing at the top is wide and sprawling with a dozen doors either side of the hallway. At the end of the passage, a huge double doorway looms—I know immediately it's Ares' master bedroom.

Entering the first room on the left, I'm surprised to see the paintwork is light, the bed central, plainly dressed with a wall of windows facing East, and a powder room adjacent. *This will be perfect.*

Turning to Ares, I say, "I'm tired from our travels. Mind if I rest here for a few hours?"

"Oh, ah, sure," he says scratching his head.

"Could you shut the door on your way out?"

I hear the door click behind me and exhale. Alone, I walk around the room and leap onto the bed—the mattress is as soft as a cocoon of feathers. My body groans at the plushness and instantly surges toward the call of sleep, while my mind fights to stay conscious. I'm asleep within seconds, my traitorous body winning the internal battle.

Raised voices downstairs rouse me from rest. I strain to hear the conversation, but all I make out is another male timbre. Jumping to the floor, I leave my self-appointed room and creep noiselessly down the spiral staircase, the heated discussion drawing me closer.

The voices are coming from deep within the depths of the fresco room so it's in that direction I forge ahead.

When I arrive, the sight that befalls me is not one I was prepared for—Hermes.

I gasp and his head pivots so quickly, I haven't time to avert my stare. "Alexandraya?"

"Hello, Hermes."

He glares at Ares and then settles his gaze back to me. "What are you doing here?"

Before I have the chance to answer, he's in front of me, left hand circling the small of my back, right hand stroking my hair, "I have missed you more than you can imagine."

Swallowing the lump wedged in my throat, I reply, "It's been a long time."

Ares cuts through the middle of the reunion. "Alexandraya is residing here for a while. Her return must be kept confidential."

"I'd like to know why my betrothed is living under your roof."

The tone of his voice has raised several decibels and he lunges toward Ares who blocks the attack, and replies, "She belongs here. You should never have let her go."

"It was a temporary measure and only while I complete errands of utmost importance. You know that."

"I know you didn't fight for her."

It's like I'm invisible. Both gods are arguing about me in front of me. This is not how I had visualised my return. Seeing Hermes was not part of the plan. Well, not in the short term.

His embrace felt like a sword stabbing at my core. Luckily, the wall of armour woven like a shield around my heart holds strong—nothing will stand in the way of my vow and my carefully laid future.

*Power is the true gift.*

"I'll leave you two to it. I'm going back to bed," I say pivoting on my heel, and using my light speed to make a quick escape.

Once back in my room, the thunderous roar of arguing echoes through the palace, followed by crashing objects, and clanging weapons. Ignoring the calamity, I slip out of my playsuit and into the shower. The cold water needles my skin and alerts my mind.

*Why did Hermes say he missed me after he had Ares deliver a message ending our partnership?*

The thought plagues my mind while I sit on the end of the bed dressed in silky black lace, dutifully gliding a brush through my dampened hair. I'm lost in theory until my attention is shifted by an incessant tapping on the bank of windows.

Perched outside is Hermes.

"What are you doing here?" I ask opening the window where he hovers.

"I had to see you."

"Why?"

"Because I love you," he replies simply.

I feel the armour crack, and curse my feeble heart. "Then why did you abandon me?"

He steps over the window sill and into my room. I take a step backward. "I would never do that Alexandraya. I told you, you are my forever—I made you a promise and I have every intention of keeping it."

"Why did you not contact me? I thought you left me."

His eyes raise, "I did. I sent Ares to tell you I would be coming for you. And I sent a letter to you at your guide parents' home advising my impending arrival. When I arrived, they informed me you were on a mission."

My legs begin to wobble, and the room starts to spin. Images of Julienne hiding a letter under her teacup emerge, and Mattias' rush to see me leave the realm crash into my mind. The realisation of what's transpired knocks the air from my lungs.

The dizziness blurs my focus and my head throbs while the duplicity of the power play at hand unravels. I should have pre-empted the tactic of a strategic god, especially one versed in war, but I was blinded by my own agenda. More fool me. Once before, I underestimated my competition and it cost me my wedding. This time, it seems Fate has unwittingly played into my hand.

*A formidable match and an easy sacrifice.*

"Are you okay, love?" Hermes says. And then he's in front of me, throwing his arms around my lingerie clad body.

His words snap me to attention, "I've never been better. In fact, I want you to leave. I've moved on and you should too," I say extracting myself from his grip.

"Alexandraya—"

"You heard the lady," Ares says from my doorway.

Hermes' face flames red as his glare meets Ares. But instead of another confrontation, he plants a kiss on my cheek. "I'll see you again soon," he says taking flight by winged sandals through the ajar window.

Ares strides to the window and slams it shut, "Are you okay?"

"I am now," I say, and slant my face up to his, flashing

him a knock out smile.

The God of War gazes at my scantily clad body, and says, "You are my dreams alive. I take what I want, and it's you that I want, Alexandraya."

"I want you to, Ares. You will make me whole."

His grin lays bare his weakness, "I will make you happy, Alexandraya. Together we will create history."

*He is not wrong.*

# CHAPTER 29

## Roman

With each new sunrise, Galena's shadow lightens. While the loss of Vincent hangs heavy, her demeanour is improving. She spends hours in the garden planting herbs and flowers, finding comfort in her former Earth Propensity. And when she finally re-enters the house after a day's labour outdoors, her hands are muddy, dirt embedded under her fingernails. More than once I've teased her about her former polished nails. But she refuses to wear gloves, saying she needs to feel the earth on her skin.

This morning she looks like a woodland nymph with her cropped hair, tiny frame, and mud stained cheeks. "What have you there?" I ask, peering into her basket.

"Dandelions," she says, her cheeks sun kissed and rosy.

Taking the harvested flowers from her basket, she proceeds to grind them in a vessel, adding pinches of clover and berries, and infusing the mixture into a pot of tea.

"Mm, that smells delicious."

She shoots me a smile, "I think it's time you left the Home Realm, Roman."

I freeze in position and answer softly, "I'm fine here for a while longer."

Reaching across the counter, she places a hand on my shoulder, "My sweet boy, you have been a pillar of strength, and I could not have managed without you. But now, while I miss Vincent desperately, I am ready to move forward with my remaining years. And it's time you went back to your training."

The newfound strength in her voice is comforting, and reassures me she'll cope without my presence. It's also how I know I can broach the subject that has been weighing on my mind, "Actually, Galena, there's something I wanted to talk to you about."

She nods while pouring two mugs of tea, "Go ahead."

Jumping straight to the point, I say, "I believe Apollo

is my god father and I'd like to go to Mount Olympus to ask him directly."

She considers my statement for a moment before answering, "How did you come to this conclusion?"

"Vincent's carving on the inside of the oak box."

"I'm not sure that's enough information to be certain. You know the Fates do not allow semi god's access to their heritage. It's forbidden for a reason—we all have our part to play in the realms. Besides, Roman, semi gods are the result of a mortal and lower deity unions."

"I think Vincent wanted me to have this information and that's why he wanted me to have the box," I say tactfully.

Staring into the living room, she gazes at the star painted ceiling. Several long seconds pass before she answers, "I know how you admire Apollo, Roman. And I don't want you jumping to unlikely conclusions. However, it does seem like Vincent left you the clue on purpose—he was always a little eccentric with his reasoning."

"That he was."

My mind drifts back to happy memories of my guide father and a sharp pang hits me in the chest.

Galena takes a sip of her tea, "I'll speak with Tyrone this afternoon and ask him to arrange for a chariot tomorrow."

While only in rare circumstances will the Realm Master order a chariot to Mount Olympus, Tyrone has always had a soft spot for Galena. In fact, most of the male population in the Home Realm do. "Thank you," I say rounding the bench and giving my guide mother a hug.

"I hope the answers you seek bring you the joy you deserve," she whispers.

******

The chariot arrives early the next morning, precisely as Galena forecasted. Behind the reins stands a deity, shorter than myself, and I instinctively straighten my posture.

"Thank you Galena."

I plant a quick kiss on the top of her head, and step into the chariot.

"Stay safe Roman, I'm always here if you need me," she says in a protective guide motherly tone.

My chest swells as the chariot takes flight, and I wave to Galena. As the horses soar skyward and the Home

Realm becomes a distant speck, I close my hand around the oak box hoping I have deciphered Vincent's message correctly. My thoughts wander back to the Passing Ceremony, and to the distant god I saw standing on the opposite bank of the Imperial Lake. Deep within my soul I know I'm right.

The journey is quick. With graceful air canters, the horses pass through the golden gates of Mount Olympus, their hooves smoothly transitioning from mid-air to solid terrain.

"I have been instructed to deliver you to Apollo's residence," the charioteer announces.

It's the first time he's spoken since I boarded the transport, and I note his cool, curt tone. Nodding, I answer, "That's correct."

The horses draw up outside the familiar palace and a wave of reminiscence hits me. Not long ago, I was here with Siriarna. At that point in time, I had no idea she was born from a pure divine bloodline. And here I am speculating that the great God Apollo is *my* father. Like a surging river, my mind runs wild with possibility of who might be my birth mother.

*Could she also be of divine blood? Am I a god like my*

*best friend?*

It's the first time I've thought about Siriarna in months, and a stab of guilt strikes me. So caught up in my own affairs, I haven't given her a thought since leaving the Sky Realm.

The chariot zips away as soon as I step from it—the deity at the helm not giving me a second glance. Striding toward the palace door, my heart hammering beneath my chest, I tell myself that my assumptions are right and Vincent left me the clue for a reason. But what if I'm wrong?

The door opens as I arrive, "Come in son," Apollo says.

*I was right! And I'm going to faint. No, I'm not—I'm going to act rationally. Apollo is my birth god. Oh my gods!*

I can hardly comprehend what is happening. My god father *is* Apollo. Vincent knew. But how? And what does this mean for me now?

"I'm sure you have many questions, Roman. Why don't you come inside, and we'll have a chat?" he says, his voice smooth and mellow.

He's right! Following behind, I have a flood of questions floating in and out of my head. When I sit on the couch that I had previously stretched out so languidly atop, I ask the one that is haunting me, "Who is my birth mother?"

My hands are clenched, and so is my jaw, as I wait for his answer. I wonder if this is how Siriarna felt when she found out her heritage. And my stomach drops just like it does when a chariot exits the Vortex. My bloodline is about to be revealed—unless he refuses to enlighten me. My heart thumps, and sweat beads at my temple.

When I stare at Apollo, his eyes are vacant. He is communicating directly with the Fates.

*What if they don't allow me my truth?*

His conscious returns as does his focus on my face, and he begins to speak... "I met your mother at a time when I was in need of great comfort."

His tone is melancholic, and his face has twisted into a grimace. If I wasn't so desperate for answers, I wouldn't push for information. But I am, so I do... "Go on."

"After a particularly brutal conflict, I escaped Mount Olympus to Pelion. I needed the solitude brought by the surrounding frosty winter. On the mountainside, I sat for days—immobile, staring ahead without focus. My mind teetering on insanity. But early on the seventh day, through the dawning misty veil blanketing the mountain, a mortal woman appeared. Her hair shone like polished silver through reflections from icicles formed on surrounding tree branches. She was as dazzling as a solitary star brightening the night sky. I was instantly captivated."

Clearing my throat and shifting on my seat, I'm ready to stop Apollo's retelling. After all, he's my father and I really don't want to hear about his tryst with my birth mother. I'm also trying to disguise the disappointment that she is mortal.

"Your mother was the most beautiful soul I have ever known. And whilst it is the duty of lower deities to reproduce with mortals to create semi gods, as you know, it is forbidden for higher gods to do the same. However, I could not resist her lure. The Fates overlooked my indiscretion, because your mother healed my shattered spirit, allowing me to continue my divine duties without bitterness. She was the one who inspired my love of music and poetry. She was everything and more."

"Was?"

It's Apollo shifting on his seat now, his eyes dewy, "I'm sorry, Roman, but your mother died during childbirth."

The air leaves my lungs, and my head becomes dizzy. I suck in a sharp breath, and another, and another, until the moment passes.

Apollo's deep-seated loss, which is now so apparent, hits me hard. Because I feel guilt that I'm glad it's Galena who lives, and not the woman who birthed me. "I'm sorry for your loss, Apollo."

"Roman, you are a ray of light, just like your mother. She asked that I watch over you until you found your path... the stormy sky you will light."

His words drift away and I'm left full of wonder. Where to next? Do I resume my training on Evolirium as if I am none the wiser to my parentage? And what effects will it have if I divulge my god father. Will it start a frenzy with the other semi gods?

"Can I stay here in the Sky Realm for a while?" I ask.

"I would like that, Roman."

# CHAPTER 30

## Siriarna

Against Apollo's advice I'm returning to Evolirium. To Braxton. It's only fair I warn him we are pawns in a battle for the ultimate overseeing power.

Using my abilities, I saturate the sky with a billow of clouds to camouflage my and Celeris' realm escape. The last living winged horse has become one of my closest allies, and together we gallop the sky as a bonded pair.

Once engulfed by the shadows and heightened altitude, I release the air from my lungs in a purgative scream. Celeris squeals in unity. However, my mouth clamps shut as soon as I spy the chariot exiting the vortex ahead.

Coaxing Celeris into a slower gait, safely obscured

behind a shield of white clouds, I lock my sight onto the chariot as it hurls past. My brows cross when I recognise Apollo's spiteful son, Oaxes, at the helm. The crease deepens when I notice standing behind him, a full head taller, is Roman.

My first instinct is to follow the duo, but despite the lure, I stroke the side of Celeris' neck and inch the horse onward. The wonder of why Roman is breaching the Sky Realm is whirled away the minute we enter the Vortex. Replaced by yearning at the pit of my stomach.

We break into Evolirium just shy of twilight. The filtered daylight and high exposure threat makes it too risky to land in the open, so I steer Celeris to the mountains. Here, from the highest peak, the view is otherworldly. Fog curls its way upward like smoky fingers grappling to rise higher against the violent gusty wind. A poignant parallel to my current circumstance.

The solitude does little to encourage optimism, but I refuse to believe my fate has been cursed forever.

Sensing the change in my aura, Celeris bobs his head and shakes his body. Dismounting, I reach into my riding coat pocket and pull out a golden apple. His tail begins to swish as his lips suck in his favourite treat.

Staring over the crystallised treetops, and through the silvery mist to the realm below, I wish for nightfall to appear. Though time moves gradually as if in spite. Forestalled by circumstance, I pace back and forth on the mountain peak, my patience beginning to fray.

It's the vibration above that averts my attention, and I glimpse Apollo in his chariot above the horizon tugging the sun from the sky.

*Finally.*

When darkness settles, I leap atop Celeris and we fly down to the meadows. Leaving the horse hidden amongst a clump of trees, I toss him another apple with instructions to remain in place.

Stepping into the meadow, my sight is focused on the semi god sitting amongst the moonflowers, and my heart beats with longing. "I wasn't sure you'd be here," I say sitting down beside him.

"Every night I show up... hoping you might return."

I've never been more desperate to collapse into his arms, but heat emanates from his tattoo reminding me of our limitations, "I couldn't stay away, even if I wanted to."

The strain of being forced apart is etched on his face,

"I thought you might be angry with me for making a vow with the Furies."

"Oh, Braxton, I am not mad. If anything, I'm glad to have my memories back."

He leans back on his elbows, "I fear my selfishness has cost us the ultimate price."

"Don't you dare say that. You kept your promise and that shows me exactly the person I already knew you were. The one I fell in love with." I lean into him, but he jerks backward maintaining a safe distance between us.

"I wish I could touch you. So damn much," he says releasing a deep sigh.

Which I mirror. Because I want him to touch me.

Instead I gaze into his eyes. The warm chestnut hue molten under the moonlight. Tempting me. Tempting Fate.

Breaking the connection, Braxton raises his head to the stars. And I begrudgingly follow his gaze. Tonight the sky is clear and the Pegasus constellation comes into view.

Celeris whinnies from his position behind the trees and the star formation blinks back. He trots, then gallops across the meadow, flapping his wings and taking flight, ascending gracefully into the sky. When he reaches the constellation, the stars twinkle in unison—two winged horses dancing in the blackened sky.

"Wow, that is quite something," Braxton says. "I thought Pegasus was one of a kind?"

"Celeris is his offspring—the last remaining winged horse in existence. He has been in hiding for centuries, protecting a cursed mortal."

"Does anyone else in the realms know of his survival?"

"Only myself, and Apollo—"

The vein in Braxton's neck pulses at the mention of Apollo. "Do you spend a lot of time with him?" he asks.

I promised myself I would never lie to him, so I answer, "He's just a friend."

Braxton shifts slightly closer and winces. Then busies himself picking clover. Now would be the perfect time to bury myself in his arms. But I can't, and I inwardly scream at the unfairness of this curse. "Do you remember the tale of Crocus?" I whisper.

Braxton draws his gaze from the trefoil, "The mortal turned flower?"

"Yes. The Fates cursed his true love for stealing ambrosia. And in retaliation, the Furies sought vengeance because they believed Crocus tricked the nymph Smilax into stealing the immortal substance. But he was innocent."

"How do you know?"

"I have met the Crocus flowers, Celeris led me to him, and he shared his memories with me. I have been trying to help him break his curse."

"Siriarna, it is not a good idea to interfere with the Furies. Trust me."

"I thought that too at first. But I can't stand by and allow a mortal to pay the ultimate price for a betrayal he did not commit. It goes against our duty to protect humanity."

It dawns on him then, "The Fates know of your plan, it's why they've placed a protection spell on you, isn't it?"

"Yes. I believe we are caught in the middle of an impending war—a fight for the ultimate overseeing power," I whisper.

He bites his nails, and his eyes drift, focussing on nothing, lost to far away thoughts. And in a tight voice, he says, "Alexandraya's vow—"

"What do you mean?" I interrupt, feeling the blood drain from my face.

He doesn't meet my eyes when he says, "In the Home

Realm, I stumbled across Alexandraya in the grasslands. She informed me we had something in common. It was after I made my vow. And she confirmed it again here on Evolirium before she left in Ares' chariot."

I should never have underestimated my cousin's thirst for power. I thought the postponement of her wedding to Hermes would quash her chance of ascension. But it seems she has found a way to reap power regardless. My mind throbs and my heart lurches.

*I need to speak with Apollo immediately.*

"I must return to Mount Olympus. I have to try and stop the mayhem before it begins. Though I fear if Alexandraya is involved, it may already be too late."

"I'm so sorry Siriarna, I didn't know I would share a Fate with Alexandraya—"

"Not a Fate, but a Fury," I say miserably.

Braxton lets out a throaty groan, "I won't fulfil my vow. Whatever they demand, I will fight it with every ounce of my being. And I promise to stay away from you."

"No Braxton, I can't lose you again. Besides, the Furies will kill you if you disobey them."

"I don't care Siriarna. I won't let any harm come to

you, and I won't be responsible for the rise of chaos."

"I care Braxton."

*I won't let you sacrifice yourself. I will fix this. We are meant to be.*

# CHAPTER 31

## Braxton

My tattoo burns as she sits beside me. But I ignore the fiery ache, because being close to her is everything—the internal scorch a mere inconvenience in comparison to the pleasure having her here ignites.

But gods how I want to touch her. To pull her into my arms and coil my hands in her hair while kissing her until we are both spent of breath. When she tells me she loves me and moves closer, I almost give in to temptation. However, the reminder of her plummeting to the earth the last time we touched, compels me to keep a safe distance between us. The restraint is torture.

To distract myself, I stare at the sky and silently wish to the Fates to help me break my vow. Even though I know they'll ignore me, I make the wish anyway. Surely they know I would never hurt Siriarna. Not intentionally.

I almost don't notice the Pegasus star constellation until the winged horse Siriarna arrived on squeals and takes flight. What a magnificent creature. Watching it frolic with the Pegasus constellation strikes me with awe. The stars blink in retort, vibrant and spirited. It's incredible, and distracts me momentarily from my dilemma.

When I ask Siriarna about the horse, she tells me Celeris is Pegasus' offspring, and has been in hiding for centuries. That's when I make the mistake of asking if anyone else knows of his existence—it's something I meant to ask the last time we were together.

Apollo. Just her, and Apollo!

I stifle the volcanic rage bubbling inside, but I can't resist asking her how much time she spends with him on Mount Olympus. Her answer is evasive, but sincere. So I shift closer until my tattoo scalds.

She whispers a story of curses by the overseeing powers that be, and the blood in my veins runs cold. After my firsthand encounter with the Furies, I can't allow them to win this war.

It seems like forever ago I made the vow to return Siriarna's memories. What a mistake. I should have known there was more at play. I kept reminding myself of her plea in the meadows before I reversed Time. That's how I justified my actions. In hindsight—

"I care, Braxton," she says.

And my heart splinters. It feels like broken shards are piercing my lungs, and my breath catches. Suddenly, I'm coughing and gasping for air.

In a flash, Siriarna is in front of me, ripping my shirt from my torso. But as her fingers graze my flesh, she is flung backward at mighty speed.

"Siriarna," I yell.

There's no response and I see her elongated body motionless on the ground ahead. Jumping to my feet I race to her, but my journey is thwarted as fire rips from my chest creating a barricade of flames.

"Siriarna!" I scream again and again.

The fire rises angrily as it quenches its thirst with surrounding oxygen. Soon, it will be unstoppable. I know I have to breach the wall, and I take a smoky breath in readiness. Then I hear her voice, "I'm okay, Braxton. Stay there," she says, predicting exactly what I'm planning.

Overhead, the tranquil night sky transforms into a picture of pure menace. Sinister charcoal clouds appear from nowhere and begin to swell. A hiss echoes before a diagonal cascade of droplets plummet to the ground, soaking the realm and the firewall in front of me.

Exposed is Siriarna now, drenched, and angry. Though her face softens when she spies me, "Thank the gods you're okay," she says.

"So, you're thanking yourself?" I manage the half-hearted joke to try and lighten her scowled expression.

"I guess I am," she jests. Though her scowl returns when she gapes at my bare seared chest.

"I'm so sorry, Siriarna."

"This is *not* your fault, Braxton. This is Fury out of control."

She's right. The Furies must be stopped. My only option is to renege my vow. There really is no choice. While my wish is to spend my life with Siriarna, I am aware hers is eternal and mine a mere cinch in her lifetime. Let Fury burn me to ashes; I won't partake in their plan.

A thunder of footsteps sounds in the distance as semi gods flee their huts. The anomaly of rain on Evolirium too alluring to ignore. Siriarna steps forward but Celeris swoops down between us.

"It's okay boy," I say holding out my palm. "I promise I won't touch your mistress."

The horse bobs his head.

"I will see you again soon, Braxton," Siriarna says mounting the equine.

"It might be best we stay apart for a while," I say, my shoulders slumping.

"Not in this lifetime," she says smiling. "Remember, I love you."

"I love you too."

And with that, she zips from the meadow, and I watch her whip through the twinkling Pegasus constellation.

*I hope she visits me when I become a star.*

\*\*\*\*\*\*

Making my back to my hut, I am bombarded with semi gods dashing along the pathway.

"Hey, Braxton, did you see the rain falling from the sky? I wonder what's going on." Sage says shifting on the spot.

"I've no idea," I reply shrugging with about as much

enthusiasm as a statue.

She doesn't wait around for further chit chat. Then I run into Davina.

"Braxton."

"Davina."

"You know, this looks like a higher power's handy work," she says smirking.

"You think?" I say noncommittedly.

"I do. And if I was a betting semi god, I'd guess you were somehow involved."

Melodie saunters up to join the two of us, "Why are you the only semi god moving in the opposite direction to the rest of us?"

They look at each other and a conspiratorial glance passes between them. "That's exactly my thought," adds Davina.

I refuse to engage, and turn my back in preparation to leave. Before I do, I hear the overly loud for-my-sake conversation. "I wonder how Alexandraya is doing in the Sky Realm," Melodie says, her voice as sweet as honeyed elixir.

The mention of Alexandraya instantly sends a razor sharp shiver down my spine. Striding forward, I don't glance back. Their sardonic laughter soon a distance trill.

But the mention of Alexandraya has my mind ticking over. In the Home Realm she revealed we were the same. While I dismissed the ludicrous claim, I'm beginning to wonder if she was referring to the furious debt.

What was her vow? And how is it linked to mine?

If there's one thing I know for certain, where Alexandraya is involved, nothing good will follow.

# CHAPTER 32

## Siriarna

The gleam from the moon is particularly luminescent this evening. Almost as if Artemis knew of my plans.

Celeris looks like a walking lantern, his alabaster coat reflecting the rays twofold. He'll be my downfall, not to mention expose himself, if we're not vigilant.

"Stay here," I whisper, settling the horse amongst the shining marble statues of the main palace tribute garden. I leave a golden apple as a parting reward, and shimmy through the statues in my midnight black clothing.

The sheen of the palace's bronze foundations act as a beacon. When I reach the stone walls, my hands find the parapet, and I hoist my body onto the golden walkway that surrounds the western side of the palace.

Creeping past the bed chambers, a shiver runs down my spine—if Hera catches me, I'll be brought before the council and likely banished. On the other hand, if Zeus catches me, I'll lose my father's trust and fracture our relationship. That thought weighs heavy. But I continue my journey past the great central hallway and fountain, past the grand dining room, and arrive at my destination—the smaller storage room adjacent to Zeus' private den.

The door is latched closed from the inside, but the window next to it sits ajar. It grinds against the stone exterior as I jostle it open. My heart pumps loudly, and I hold my breath, which only serves to heighten the sound of my pulse ringing through my ears. The palace remains still despite the clatter, and I take my cue, squeezing myself through the window gap into the storage room.

Prowling through the dimness into the hallway, my darkly clad silhouette is cloaked by the shadows. I glance over my shoulders, and satisfied by my aloneness, enter the den. The air is thick and heavy, like a veil laden with authority and power. There is no doubting this is Zeus' private sanctuary. Slivers of moonlight through the highline window provide enough light for this evening's objective—although, I pause momentarily at the inset bookshelves.

I force myself away from the tomes and dart behind the grand oak desk. With trembling fingers, I open the drawer. There are two compartments separated by a timber divider. One compartment houses trinkets and artefacts. And the other, a stack of papers. Gathering the pile, I flick through the contents. Nothing stands out as highly confidential nor mysterious.

As I replace the papers, my fingers skim a latch at the back of the compartment. Excitement wells in the pit of my stomach as I click the latch. A secret drawer lurches forward containing a singular parchment.

My mouth dries when I read the lettering… "The seed of destruction is sprouting. Time is slipping away."

I stare at the words for what seems like an eternity until I hear the sound of approaching footsteps. Shoving the parchment back into place, I quickly close the drawer and dive beneath the desk.

The door of the den swings open and I feel the blood freeze in my veins.

"Who's there?" comes a familiar voice.

I stand and reveal myself, "It's me Bia."

"What in the realms are you doing in here, Siriarna?"

I think about withholding the reason for my intrusion, but I trust Bia with all my soul. "A war is coming Bia, and I thought Zeus might have information that could help solve the puzzle."

*I won't let Braxton pay the price.*

She nods her head. "I've heard whispers in the hallways. But I don't understand why you wouldn't just ask your father, instead of stealing? He would be most disappointed if he found out," she says protectively.

"I know. I didn't want to cause panic. And the last time I asked for his help, he said he wouldn't interfere with matters regarding curses, nor overseeing deities. And Bia, I think this has everything to do with curses, especially the Furies."

"Oh Siriarna, what have you gotten yourself into?"

"I stumbled upon Crocus in the woodlands. He needs my help Bia, I'm his only hope."

Her tone softens, "You are truly a divine soul, Siriarna. But curses are not to be messed with. The consequences are never worthy of the sacrifice."

"It's a risk I have to take. Especially if a war is looming."

*And Alexandraya is no doubt at the heart of it.*

Her head swivels back and forth, and she whispers, "Someone's coming, you have to get out of here. Now."

Panic rises as I realise I'm trapped, "I came through the storage room," I say.

"You won't be leaving that way," she says matter-of-factly. "Through the window, it's the only way."

She rushes forward and boosts me to the highline window. I give it an almighty shove and topple through the opening, "...nothing to worry about," I hear Bia say as I fall.

Certain I'm going to smack into the ground, I brace for impact. But Celeris flies to my rescue, catching me on his back, and soars us into the evening sky.

"Thank you, boy," I say stroking his mane.

# CHAPTER 33

## Alexandraya

From the doorway, I glance back at Ares and note the rhythmic pattern of his breathing—the God of War looks so peaceful. I bite down on my lip until it bleeds to stop myself from laughing at the irony. The familiar metallic scent and salty taste a comforting reminder of the trials that have led me to this pivotal moment. Ascension beckons from the shadows, and I have never been more prepared.

Giddy, I sashay down the hallway in a floaty cream chiton, my mood as light as the feathery soft material. The glow through the palace windows from the smattering of stars, naturally lights my pathway.

In the sanctuary of my room a glint from outside the

window catches my eye, and I move to the source. There, on the window sill, lies a perfectly formed red rose. My heart begins to thrash like a caged beast, and I have to use every ounce of self-control to ease it back to its normal beat. Against better judgement, I open the window and retrieve the flower. The scent is hypnotising, and instantly transports me into the Hermes' conservatory.

*My conservatory.*

Rushing to the bed I grab a pillow and shove it over my mouth to stifle the mounting scream. Once expelled, regaining my composure is somewhat easier. Reaching into my satchel, I pull out my second last bindweed berry and swallow. "Smilax, are you there?"

Her voice echoes through my mind, "Of course, Alexandraya. Is everything alright?"

"Yes. Now I'm back on Mount Olympus, I thought it prudent we go over the plan a final time," I say seeking the distraction, even though I have fine-tuned every last detail.

The rustle of leaves echoes her excitement. Just as it should. "Okay, let's begin," she hums.

When Smilax's voice eventually fades, simultaneously with the rising sun, my mind is cleansed, and my focus returned.

Taking the rose to the bathroom, I place it in a vessel and fill it with water. Out of immediate sight, but not completely out of the picture.

The tang of the bindweed berry remains on my lips and my stomach growls. I'm famished. I haven't eaten in a week. While I could push my hunger further, in accordance with the trial of abstinence, my destiny now belongs to me. And it warrants a celebratory feast.

Down the spiral stairs I trail in search of the palace kitchen. There is a severe lack of natural light in the lower level palace fortress, and as I pass the fresco room, I swear the animals depicted are following me with their realistic painted eyes. It's rather creepy. Quickening my step, I continue my hunt for food.

Beyond the study, that looks more like a war room armoury with maps and weapons, I find the kitchen. It's large and plain, but there is a large window that provides a flare of natural daylight. At the far end is a cobbled arch with a solid timber latched door. Curiosity piqued, I'm drawn forward. I can't resist the temptation to open it, so I give a mighty shove, and the door creaks open. And what I'm confronted with is not what I expected—a steep staircase leading downward.

Logically, I follow the flight of stairs.

The air is thick and stale the further I travel, and the light from the opened doorway fades the further I descend. To add to the excitement rising in my stomach, instead of using my Propensity power to light the way, I extend my hands so they caress both walls, and continue to step down in the darkness. When I reach the bottom, I create a miniature light source with my Propensity power—a candle in my palm. In front of me, the flickering light unveils a wall to wall iron-barred cell.

"I see you've found my dungeon."

Pivoting to face Ares, I smile, and say, "It's magnificent."

His obsidian eyes shine wide, "It doesn't frighten you?"

"On the contrary, I find it comforting."

"Alexandraya, you were born to be my match," he growls.

*Never truer words spoken.*

My stomach picks this moment to unabashedly rumble. Ares let's out a throaty laugh, "Let's get you something to eat, my petite warrior."

Up the staircase we climb, and into filtered daylight we return. It takes me a moment to readjust my sight to the brightness, and I shield my eyes with the back of my hand. When they adapt to the change of setting, I see Ares pouring some kind of mixture into a stoneware mug, "For strength," he says, handing me the smoky elixir.

Pressing the strange concoction to my lips, I sip. Umami flavoured liquid slides down my throat, and my stomach backflips. It is unexpectedly tasty, and the smoky scent lingering behind warms my senses, and satisfies my hunger. "Amazing," I say surreally.

"Perfect before battle," he discloses pompously. "I keep a supply on hand."

His eyes rake my body slowly, lingering on the material cinched at my waist where his enormous hands gripped me tightly last night. Whilst not the worst experience, sex with Ares is perfunctory. He loves like he fights... methodically. I don't plan a repeat experience.

Airily I say, "It's time I roam this magnificent palace you've created."

"The palace is not going anywhere, perhaps we should take more time to explore each other?" he says with fire in his eyes.

*Not if I can help it.*

"That's true," I say with a laugh. "But I'd hate to be the one who drags you away from your preparations," I say, hoping the strewn maps across the war room are more worthy of his attention.

He groans, "You're right, I do have some urgent business to take care of. I'll see you at sundown."

"Perfect."

"Alexandraya."

"Yes?"

"Stay on palace grounds."

The possessive instruction grates on my nerves. Although, perhaps warranted given last night's conflict with Hermes. "Of course," I reply.

He bends down and kisses me on the lips, firm and assertive, "Thank you, petite."

The reference makes me cringe, but I plaster a smile across my face, and waltz from the room. My chiton swishes across the floor in time with my thundering heartbeat.

In the open space outside the palace, I gulp a few mouthfuls of fresh air grateful to escape Ares' clutches. The pristine lawn wraps around the high perched palace, and I start my exploration in the opposite direction of south.

A shadowed pattern on the ground in front of me raises my sight skyward. Above glides a vulture.

Watching.

Stalking.

Irritation swells, and when I approach a maze of perfectly manicured hedges, I take my chance at losing the unwelcome tail.

Like the palace, the maze is a fortress. Thick forest green shrubbery knits together forming solid perimeter walls. Down the labyrinth I travel—broad daylight becoming filtered splintered rays the further I go.

Soon I reach the first junction. Instinctively, I choose the left pathway and continue my journey, ensuring my hand is in constant contact with the wall. The leaves are criss-crossed by spiky branches—a subtle warning to maze entrants, but not enough of a deterrent to stop my touch.

At the next intersection I turn right and continue moving forward, eventually arriving at an enclosed dead end. Frustration knits my brow, and a brusque snarl leaves my throat.

Retracing my steps, I turn left. And when I reach the

next junction, I make another left turn. The pathway ahead remains unobstructed. This is the moment I solve Ares' maze. Left is the right way out. Methodical, precise, predictable.

With no intention of returning to the palace before nightfall, I leisurely saunter through the privet until Apollo tows the sun from the realm and Artemis brings forth the moon.

Ares is pacing the fresco room when I return to the palace, his face as ruddy as his tunic. "Where have you been? I have been searching for you," he spits. "I specifically instructed you not to leave the palace grounds."

"I've been in the maze. I was quite overwhelmed with its complexity," I lie.

"Of course it is challenging, my petite." He lifts my chin and speaks slowly, "Thank you for abiding by my rules. They are to keep you safe... from Zeus, and Siriarna."

The mention of my cousin steals my breath for a split second. While I look forward to the moment we meet in person, now is not that time. "Thank you for watching over me," I reply without blinking.

*Like a vulture.*

"I will remedy the injustice. We will unite post-haste."

"That moment can't come quick enough," I say, licking my lower lip. His promised partnership fuelling my desire aspiration.

Ares swoops down, covering my mouth with his, "I have a Council Meeting now, and will ensure it's without delay. Wait for my return—"

"Of course," I interrupt before he can finish his sentence.

*Absolutely, I won't.*

Returning to my room, I shut the door and click the latch to lock—then, breathe out a victorious sigh. There will be no union tonight.

Impulsively, I walk to the window and discover another perfect red rose laying on the sill, its ruby shade accentuated by the moonlight. A single drop of evening dew clings stubbornly to a petal, and when I lift the flower into my hand, moisture drips in surrender.

Adding the flower to the vessel in the bathroom, I'm struck by the synergy of both roses. Time to end this. Two is indeed company, three an unnecessary crowd.

# CHAPTER 34

## Alexandraya

At last, it's my time. I'm certain this morning's predawn glow is a rosy gift and divine sign. And when I hear the impatient banging on my door, I'm ready for what lies beyond.

"Good morning Ares," I sigh, stifling a fake yawn when opening the oak barrier.

His eyes glide over my figure from head to toe, "Aren't you a vision," he says taking note of my scant underwear. "I missed you last night!"

Forcing a lazy smile and ignoring the innuendo, I ask, "How did your Council Meeting go?"

"It was everything I promised you."

My stomach lurches and heat courses through my

veins, "When?" I ask in a barely controlled tone. The last time I was to be married, it was postponed for a year and it's hard to imagine he succeeded in his feat.

"Today."

His face is pure triumph. A look that implies he's won the war. And for his part, he has. "I can't believe Zeus agreed... and so quickly."

He smirks when he replies, "Not Zeus. Hera. Hera will officiate our union, and will bring ambrosia for your transformation afterwards."

A genuine smile lights up my face.

*Queen takes King.*

Everything is in place.

"You are a supreme God, Ares," I breathe. "My God."

He growls.

I hook my fingers into the tiny lace barely concealing my flesh, and slide it to the floor. After all, everyone deserves one final moment of bliss.

******

Lying in the aftermath of my valedictory gift, a tempest of wind howls up the stairs and flays the solid oak bedroom door around like a sheet of paper, disturbing the silence.

Ares jumps from my bed, throws on his robe, and flees my room in a sizzling rage.

Following his lead, I dress quickly and fight my way downstairs through the blustering gale. When I arrive, Hermes is standing in the vestibule, caduceus raised, Psyche trailing behind. He lowers the staff, and the internal palace whirlwind surrenders. His eyes flick briefly my way, but swiftly return their lock on Ares who is circling him like a rabid dog hunting its prey.

"That's quite enough," Psyche commands.

Ares ignores the instruction and continues to stalk my former partner.

"What are you two doing here?" I ask in a tone that matches my steely expression.

"I've come to take you home," Hermes replies indignant.

"I told you it was over, Hermes. I don't want you. This *is* my home."

He recoils as if I've slapped him across the face. True, the words are harsh, much harsher than intended. But I cannot afford any obstacles now, I'm too close to my divine destiny.

"You don't mean that. I *know* you Alexandraya."

My legs wobble. Ever so slightly, but they wobble. And Psyche spies the flinch. Pressing my fingernails into my palm, the tingle of punctured flesh reminds me to hold firm. "I'd like you to leave."

Ares ceases to prowl and moves to my side, circling my waist with his arm. The pressure is more than firm, and I feel my ribs bruise from his touch, but I hold my posture rigid. "That is the second time my partner has asked you to leave. I won't be held responsible if you make it a third."

Hermes' eyes narrow to a squint at the mention of *partner*, and his grip on caduceus tightens. Battle lines are drawn. He raises the staff, but before he can slam it to the marble floor, Psyche flutters in front of him and halts the movement mid-air. Then she glares at Hermes, projecting her soul of calmness over him, and says, "It's time to leave."

"You have made a grave misjudgement, Alexandraya. And you have made a boundless enemy, Ares," Hermes says, casting a steely glare.

Never has a message been so vehemently received.

*You will forgive me. You must.*

261

A dust storm whips through the palace door as he resentfully retreats by winged sandals. Dirt catches in my throat, and I begin to cough in uncontrollable bursts.

"Get some water, Ares," Psyche demands.

He rushes away, returning seconds later with a vessel of water which I snatch and I gulp. The liquid relieves the grit from my throat and my breathing returns to normal.

"Better, petite?"

My teeth gnash together, but I manage a weak smile, "Much."

"Psyche, we have business to tend to. You can leave now," Ares says stonewalling the true nature of what is about to happen.

"Alexandraya, can see me out."

His arms cross his body, and he remains poised in position. With Psyche not moving, he finally recedes and stalks down the hallway, straight into his study.

Now that he's no longer in sight, Psyche begins, "Alexandraya, what for the life of the Fates, are you doing here?"

The feeling of someone watching sends a shiver down my spine, and I look over my shoulder. On the wall behind me hangs a monochrome fresco, blending seamlessly into the palace walls. The charcoal outline of a vulture merges faultlessly into the cloudy scape, its yellow eyes the only stand out feature—remarkably lifelike. Turning my gaze back to my Aunt, I say, "I'm exactly where I should be, Psyche."

Her wings flutter rapidly as she speaks, "You are playing with fire. Hermes does not take kindly to embarrassment. Especially, when he has pledged his loyalty to you. And you have thrown it in his face."

"It's a matter of interpretation," I reply.

"I forbid you to continue down this path. There is still a chance you can mend your relationship with Hermes. I will support your plea."

Something inside me snaps. "With due respect Psyche, you are *not* my mother. I will do as I wish, and I've made my choice. It's best you heed Ares' request and leave."

Without another word, my Aunt retreats, her beautiful translucent wings changing to a menacing pitch-black.

# CHAPTER 35

## Siriarna

Celeris waits agitated on the front grass, his sixth sense charging his mood, while I storm Apollo's palace door. My hair hangs loosely in last night's braid, and I'm still wearing the black riding pants I fell asleep in—although, I did manage to throw on a fresh indigo top.

The face that greets me when the door opens is not what I expect... Roman. He pulls me into a hug, "Siriarna, I've missed you," he says ruffling my hair, his stature taller again than the last time I saw him.

*Hmm, when was that? It seems a lifetime ago.*

"What are you doing here?"

"Don't sound so excited to see me," he says frowning.

"Of course I'm happy to see you. It's just that I have

urgent business with Apollo," I say rotating my head so his hands fall away.

As I shift, he spies Celeris, and his jaw drops, "You rode a winged horse? I thought the breed died with Pegasus."

*If I had a wish for every time I've heard that lately.*

"He has been in hiding for centuries, though is becoming a less kept secret," I respond, rolling my eyes.

"Since when do we have secrets?"

He runs his left hand through his hair, his tell. And I instantly know he's hiding his own. "We don't. Well, we wouldn't have if—"

"... we hung out." He finishes my sentence.

Nodding, a wave of nostalgic remorse hits me. But I've no time for reminiscing, and I shuffle from foot to foot.

"It's okay, Siriarna," he says quietly. "I'll get my... Apollo."

"I'm right here," booms Apollo's voice.

Roman steps aside to reveal a very tense looking Apollo. "Siriarna, what's going on?"

I glance at Roman, and decide I've had enough of keeping secrets, "It's Alexandraya—she has made a gods-awful choice."

"What do you mean?" Roman says, his face full of

concern.

Apollo's eyes ignite... "*She's* the link! The seed of destruction. The one who will wreak havoc on the realm."

"Whoa, easy does it. I'm sure you're mistaken," Roman says protectively.

Apollo shakes his head, "I'm afraid I'm not. The war is imminent."

My power begins to crackle through my veins as the words on the parchment in Zeus' secret desk compartment barge their way to the forefront of my mind. Thanks to Braxton, I knew Alexandraya had made a furious vow, but I did not know she was quite literally the seed of destruction. Although, knowing my cousin and her thirst for power at any cost, I'm not sure why this surprises me. "It's time we informed Zeus of these developments. If a war is coming, he should be aware Alexandraya is at the centre of it."

"Wait!" yells Roman. "You don't know for certain that she is involved." His tone is desperate, and his face is filled with concern.

I feel my face flush red, but before I lash out at him with words I cannot take back, a rush of wind blows through my braid.

Turning, I come face to face with my mother. Both Apollo and Roman automatically shift either side of me, Alexandraya temporarily forgotten.

"What can I do for you Psyche?" Apollo breaks the silent standstill.

"We need to speak," she replies.

On closer inspection, her furiously flapping wings are tarnished. Her face is just as dark. "How about I take Roman back to Evolirium and leave you two to it?" I offer, keen to escape the confrontation.

Roman shoots me a livid glare, but I ignore him because I know he will be much safer away from this realm.

"This concerns you too, Siriarna. Though it does not concern the semi god." Psyche's voice drips with disdain when referring to Roman.

"We'll convene in my den. Roman, would you mind waiting in the parlour?" Apollo asks. His voice is filled with care, quite the opposite of my mother's.

Roman nods, and I smile at him in a way that I hope conveys a kind of peace offering. Then I follow my mother and Apollo.

As soon as we enter the den, Psyche blurts, "Trouble is

brewing for Alexandraya. She is under Ares' whim. Though I feel her soul is conflicted. That is why I've come to you Apollo—"

"She is Fury incarnate, Ares would be wise to steer clear," I say. And, as I speak the words, a haze of red wafts before my eyes.

"Siriarna, whilst we have had our...difficulties, we are family," she says a little too aggressively.

*Family! Her niece is the seed of destruction and I am the seed of her guilty past.*

Thunder growls from above.

Apollo places a hand on my shoulder, and instantly the storm subsides.

"We need to put a stop to whatever Ares is planning, otherwise I fear Alexandraya will lose the essence of her spirit," Psyche continues, her blackened wings still beating wildly.

*Where was this concern when my soul was in danger? And though his egotism is obnoxious, it's Ares' wellbeing I'm worried about, not Alexandraya's.*

Apollo's eyes glaze over, and he falls to his knees, temporarily leaving corporeal form. Then he yelps in pain, gripping his head between his hands.

Footsteps pound the hallway as Roman charges into the den. "What's happening?" he says rushing to Apollo, cradling his slumped body against his shoulder.

Both Psyche and I join Roman, kneeling on the floor beside the God of Light who looks very much unilluminated, our animosity temporarily forgotten.

Apollo tries to stand but falls back to his knees, "The Fates, they have shared a premonition. Alexandraya is about to shun her Fate and seal her Fury," he says breathlessly.

"NO," Psyche shrieks.

"Only you can stop the anarchy Siriarna. You alone," he says, eyes locking mine.

The curlicue on my arms begins to pulse; the tattoo of Fate illuminating my skin.

Psyche's wings propel her forward and she covers my hands in hers. I'm about to snatch them away, but when I glare at her, anguish is written across her perfect heart-shaped face. "It appears you have a great burden to carry," she whispers, and her wings begin to shed their sable.

*Does she not know? Is she that oblivious? Weight is all I carry.*

Apollo interrupts the peculiar moment, "There is no

269

time to spare. Vows will be collected," he says with raised brows.

My heartbeat thrashes inside my ribcage as I'm reminded of Braxton's oath to the trio of vengeful powers. If he refuses their order, they'll kill him or worse... curse him.

Images of the Crocus flowers fill my mind, and a fresh kind of agony gnaws at my soul. Cracking thunder fills the realm and a downpour of rain weeps from the sky.

"*You* can put a stop to this, Siriarna. You are protected by the Fates." Apollo's says, his speech coming in strained tones.

He's right. His words snap me to response. I was born for this moment, spared by the higher power, and it's time to fulfil my purpose. My destiny is calling. The rain subsides as I rein in my power, just as Zeus taught me during the countless hours of training at the main palace. "It's time."

Apollo grins. No words leave his mouth. And his head sags as if his shoulders cannot bear its weight.

"Help him," Roman yells desperately.

I rush forward but Psyche blocks my path. "I will take Apollo to the main palace. To Zeus," she says. "You have a destiny to fulfil, Siriarna. Go."

Apollo uses his almighty strength to hoist his head upright. His pale blue eyes dart around the room, and come to rest on Roman's identical pair. Then he says through jagged breaths, "Roman, you must lower the sun in all realms before Artemis raises the moon. If you don't, the combined luminosity will blind all that inhabit the realms. Acteon and Lampos will guide you."

Psyche speaks up, "Only your descendants can helm the golden chariot."

"Roman," Apollo says as firmly as he is able.

"I will do it, father."

# CHAPTER 36

## Alexandraya

The minute Psyche leaves, Ares appears by my side. Stroking my hair he says, "It's time to ready ourselves. Hera will soon arrive."

My well-practiced smile gleams under his scrutiny, "I'll be but a moment."

His speech trails away as my Light speed exit carries me to my room and straight to my window. The sill is bare. Thumping disappointment pounds my chest, but it is quickly replaced with the strum of victory. After all, I am mere moments away from a destiny carved by my own hand.

I squeeze myself into a figure hugging emerald dress and slip the filigree emerald ring onto my index finger—*I promise to return to you.* Then I brush my hair into straight perfection, and tuck one of the red roses Hermes previously left on my window sill behind my right ear.

*If only you could witness my finest hour.*

Before leaving my room, I fasten the red cape around my shoulders, and retrieve the last bindweed berry from my satchel. Squashing it between my fingers, I apply a generous layer of the red berry paste to my lips.

I'm ready.

My stomach swirls with unequivocal anticipation as I descend the palace staircase. The timing must be precise—between Apollo setting the sun and Artemis raising the moon.

Ares is waiting in the fresco room, dressed is his finest war wears—sword sheathed at his waist and shield pinned to his side. He turns when I hover in the open doorway, "You will make a grand goddess indeed. The perfect complement to my epithet."

"I will ensure you grow to your fullest potential."

His chest puffs at the praise.

The knock at the palace door catches my breath. If Psyche or Hermes stand beyond, my timeline will be severely compromised.

Ares strides to the door, head held high, and reefs it open revealing Hera. My sigh of relief is instant. She is dressed in an identical red cape with a crown atop her head. Her nod of approval at my wears lifts my spirits.

Ares' brows knit as he looks from Hera to me.

"Alexandraya, I'm pleased you are wearing the gift I bestowed."

"I appreciate your thoughtfulness," I reply and bow my head.

Ares beams and puffs out his chest at the exchange between the goddess and me.

"My chariot awaits," she says leading the way to the unexpected, but enchanting transport.

Replacing horses at the chariot helm, is a proud standing peacock, its spectacularly iridescent tail fanning behind. Preening. Watching.

Hera's magical creatures are legendary, and experiencing part of her stable first hand is as remarkable as I have so many times imagined.

Ares steps into the chariot first and lowers the ladder. Each step I take feels like a divine ascent.

When Hera takes the helm, the peacock lowers its tail and takes flight.

Soon after, we arrive at the veil shielding Antress. My heart beats double pace as the chariot lands at the place where my destiny foretold.

"Where are we?" Ares asks.

"A sacred enclave, perfect for what is to unfold," Hera answers stoically.

I place my hand in Ares' and squeeze, "My love, thank you for what you are about to bestow."

His ego distracts his curiosity, and he wraps his arms around me and leans down to kiss my lips.

Laughing, I pull away, "You must wait for the moment we unify."

"As you wish, petite." He offers his arm, and though I internally cringe, outwardly I graciously take it.

Hera nods to the peacock who fans out its tail in all its glory. Then, she leads the way through the veil and into the depths of the grotto. My sanctuary. My saviour.

"You're here?" Smilax's voice rings through my mind.

Gnashing my lips together, I reply, "As promised."

"Are you ready?" she asks.

"I have never been more ready."

The central inky pool is lit by dozens of tiny candles floating on top of water lilies. At the side, a wooded alter nestles amongst the bindweed. Ares' grip on my arm tightens when he realises where we are. "Smilax?" he hisses.

"Who?"

"A cursed nymph. There are many prophecies surrounding the bindweed, Alexandraya. This is a dangerous place to be."

I lock my eyes onto his and smile, "Does the chaos not excite you?"

He scans the space from the central pool to the rocky walls covered in twisted vines, and rests momentarily on the exit. Preparing his strategy. Preparing for an unforeseen war. Then he licks his lips and replies, "It does."

Fireworks explode within my mind, a victory of colour, and I can't tell if they stem from me or Smilax.

The joy is temporarily stalled by the sun dipping in jagged movements across the sky, most unlike its usual poetic departure. A vague sense of familiar creeps over my soul, but is quashed by Smilax who hums into my thoughts.

Hera clears her throat. And Ares, picks up my left hand, squeezing it between his. My eyes wince, but Hera ignores the flinch, and pulls the hood of her cloak over her head. It's time.

"Today, I have great pleasure in uniting Ares and Alexandraya—"

"What's wrong, Hera?" Ares' asks at the pause.

"Siriarna, she is here to destroy your union," she says, her face twisting into a seethe of anger.

The bindweed leaves quiver, and the berries hanging from their stems begin to drop violently, staining the ground in blood red splotches.

My blood runs cold.

*Not again.*

As predicted, appearing from the narrow entrance, is Siriarna. Her face is as ominous as the indigo of her clothing. "Alexandraya. You must stop the ceremony," she demands.

"Stay out of this cousin." I warn.

Ares' gasp is palpable, "You're related?" He drops my hand, and I feel my heartbeat still, along with my breath.

Siriarna takes another step forward, closing the distance between us, "You will start an unstoppable war. I cannot allow it." She looks from me to Hera, her face strained with anger.

"Help," I plead in a voice that sounds foreign in my mind.

"Sisters, I call to you," Hera booms.

And the Furies respond.

Candles scatter violently, and the water in the central pool divides in an inky upsurge. From deep within the watery ravine, the three Furies rise and stand atop the pool, serpents hissing at their waists, the hood of their red capes covering their crown.

It's the moment I realise my icy sanctuary is actually a connection to the River Styx, and a direct link to the underworld. The final pieces of the puzzle combine. My vow, my role in this divine tussle, I am allegiant to Fury. For eternity. And the promise of power warms my blood.

The three entities step across the water in glided movements, and position themselves in the space between Hera, Ares and me, and Siriarna. Ruthless smiles adorn their faces, and moments later Braxton is summoned, appearing at their side.

Siriarna screams and Braxton reaches for her, but one Fury holds him back with a claw like grip, and whispers in his ear. He shakes his head and releases the most gods awful noise I've ever heard, before falling to his knees.

Gradually he stands, and with his head lowered, he brings the Ribbons of Time to his hand. Then he twists in such a melancholic rhythm, a hum of sorrow vibrates in his palm. And standing like a statue is Siriarna... Time frozen, arms outstretched, a single tear clinging to her cheek.

For a semi god, Braxton's power is truly remarkable.

Ares' battle sense causes him to draw his sword. "We're leaving, Alexandraya," he says tugging at my arm.

Smilax's cries shoot through my mind.

It's not over... I will fulfil my destiny.

Freely, I step forward into the blade, its tip slashing through the right side of my lower abdomen.

*The trial of endurance.*

The God of War drops the hilt, and the sword clangs to the ground. "What have I done?" he says in a feathery voice.

"I'm okay," I say, swaying on my feet, my breaths coming in razor sharp succession.

"You're bleeding and you are not yet immortal." His face is the picture of concern. I almost feel a hint of remorse.

His arms extend, but my knees buckle, and I collapse

backwards.

At lightning speed, Ares' circles my shoulders with his arms, cradling my head before it hits the ground. "Thank you," I whisper, squeezing a tear from my fluttering eyelashes.

"Stay with me, Alexandraya," he says, before pressing his lips to mine, trying to breathe life into my dying body.

It's the moment I've been waiting for.

My hands scratch at the ground beside me frantically searching for the sword. When my hands finally stumble upon the cool metal, I gather the weapon into my shaking hands and plunge it into the top of Ares' back. His eyes widen, and then roll into the back of his skull. And I manoeuvre myself out of the way as his body crashes to the ground beside me.

The bindweed berry transferred through our lips is now mixed with his blood.

*"The blood of a god will release me."*

A tempest of wind blasts through the grotto and the bindweed vines peel away from the cave walls like a snake shedding it skin. Though my vision starts to wane as my body verges on unconscious, I watch Smilax transform into corporeal form in front of me. Her long, curly auburn hair spills over her shoulders, untamed and as wild as the vine she once was. "Thank you Alexandraya you did, indeed keep your promise." And then she turns to Hera, "Are you ready?"

Hera kneels down beside Ares' lifeless body and says, "I'm sorry, son. This was the only way to assume control—it's my time now. You will be honoured for your sacrifice. For today marks the day Fate has been undone by the will of Fury."

As my final breaths come in shallow spurts, the Furies form a circle around my body. The three clasp hands, and chant in a low macabre tone. A spirit of fiery smoke swirls above me and then flitters downward, hovering above my mouth. Red capes nod and with all the strength I can summon, I open my jaw and swallow the offering.

In one swift, sharp movement, the entities return to the central pool from which they came, and disappear beneath the inky surface.

Heat floods through my body as the ingested smoke settles in my veins. My limbs stretch and my height increases. And my already flawless skin and gleaming hair takes on a luminescence reserved for the immortal. Ares' power is now mine. The power I was promised when I proffered my vow.

I am, at last, a God.

Alexandraya... Goddess of War.

******

As my destiny unfolds, so does Ares'.

The earth below my feet begins to rumble, and a sharp and deafening crack follows as the earth separates. In an instant, Ares' body is swallowed by the chasm. Vines spring from his final resting place, their tendrils winding like a labyrinth up the rock face. He has adopted Smilax's fated curse and will remain in botanical form for all eternity.

"Return to your palace, Alexandraya. I will come for you soon," Hera orders.

"As you wish," I reply, dizzy with realisation.

*My palace.*

Then Hera and Smilax—who shoots me a smile I can only describe as liberated—vanish into the depths of River Styx's tributary with a hallowed splash and allegiance of Fury.

Sensing the imminent departure, the vine beside me

rustles in the emerging wind, and I hear a word muffled and gruff... "Help."

I stroke the coarsely toothed oval leaves, and whisper, "You were right, Ares... together we have, indeed, made history."

The leaves shake like a feather caught in a violent storm, then sprout a cluster of plump and juicy blackberries. While tempting, I will not be fooled into tasting the spoils of war. "Rest well, you have battled hard, but it's my time now. And as you can see, I am no longer petite."

Moonlight becomes the only source of light as the candles across the pond wink out one by one. As I exit Antress for the last time, I come face to face with my cousin. The satisfaction of her being oblivious to my rise into divinity, brings a huge grin to my face.

*Let the battle begin.*

"You will not get away with this, Alexandraya."

It's Braxton. His words are filled with venom, and his face is the picture of pure hate. I guess it's understandable, given the circumstances. "I already have, thanks to you. And you may call me Goddess Alexandraya." The words feel like silk on my lips. And raise the question of what almighty gifts come with my newly acquired immortality.

Clearing my mind, I subliminally reach deep into my core and locate where Ares' power rests. My power. And what I discover is truly remarkable. In utter glee, I transform myself into a vulture and take flight. My feathered arms glide through the sky, flapping with powerful movements, lifting me toward the horizon. It takes a moment for my eyes to adjust to their sharpened vision, and once they do, I peer below into the grotto from where I came. That's when I spot Braxton bringing the Ribbons of Time to his palm, and a brief wave of panic plagues my mind. I can't let him reverse Time and destroy what has been set in place.

Swooping down, talons extended, I hook my claws into his back and soar into the sky. The additional weight rips at my newly healed stomach wound, but I suppress the pain and fly onwards.

His body slumps against my grip, and I know he's resigned to his fate. The Fate of Fury.

# CHAPTER 37

## Roman

Panic pours into my stomach as I watch my father falter. I can't lose him like I did Vincent. I can't. As I cradle his head in my lap, my chest aches, but I won't let him down. I've made a promise to set the sun, and I intend on honouring it. Under any other circumstance, this responsibility would be a dream come true. Not this time. Watching him grip his head concerns me. Though immortal, the fact that the Fates are communicating so violently, has me questioning *his* very fate.

Siriarna's eyebrows shoot upward when she discovers Apollo is my god father. Psyche's too. There's no time to explain, we both have our own personal missions to complete. An instant understanding passes between us, and we silently make our way outside the palace—she to the winged horse she arrived on, and me to the golden chariot.

Acteon and Lampos whinny as I approach, no doubt intrigued as to why their master is absent at sunset phase. "You're stuck with me today," I say in a low voice. Two sets of deep brown eyes stare, sizing me up. "I know, but together we will rest the sun. I need you two to guide me."

They neigh their response and I step into the chariot. Trotting from their quarters across the lawn, they increase speed to a canter, and then gallop until their hooves no longer touch the earth. We are airborne in seconds, the horses' routine well practiced and succinct.

As we approach, I remember the moment when Apollo took me on this exact expedition. Back then, I declined the opportunity to rope the brilliant shining star. A stab of guilt strikes my soul when I remember the wish I made.

*This is not what I wanted, not in this way.*

The horses approach their accustomed position, and wait for me to fulfil my duty. With shaking hands, I reach down and grab the golden lasso coiled on a hook at the front of the chariot. Then I throw it with all my might toward the glowing orb in front of me and wish to the Fates that it successfully lands.

It doesn't.

The horses' hooves buck mid-air, and I struggle to keep the chariot in position while reeling in the empty rope. "Easy," I say in the most soothing tone I can muster.

Acteon and Lampos obey and still their movement.

Taking a deep breath, I raise the lasso above my head and twirl the golden rope, releasing it on a silent count of three. By the miracle of Light itself, it loops its target. My chest swells with reverberating aftershock, and my body is saturated with bright unadulterated light. The feeling is phenomenal and my soul hums in enchantment. The elation washing through my being loosens my grip on the lasso, and the sun begins to slip. Bracing myself against the wall of the chariot, I yank the daylight upward and tighten my hold on the bind, regaining some semblance of control.

As the chariot speeds over the horizon, sun trailing jerkily behind, a reflection catches the corner of my eye. Below, in a secluded grotto, I spy the culprit—jet black hair, shiny as a tinted mirror... Alexandraya.

After tucking the sun into its divine resting place, I

deviate Acteon and Lampos toward the grotto instead of returning them to the stables at my father's palace. And whilst they initially buck their disagreement at the change of routine, they eventually give in to my gentle coaxing.

Landing the horses a safe distance away, I ease them toward the grotto at a slower than normal gait. When I discover a concealed space behind a jutting rock shelf, I navigate the golden chariot into position and coil the reins around the ledge.

Creeping with noiseless steps toward the entrance, I glimpse a peacock, tail fanned. Careful not to disturb its line of vision, I cloak my presence behind a mass of vines and hanging berries, and slip into the grotto.

My vision finds Alexandraya immediately. She is wearing a brilliant vivid emerald dress, and a red cape. She has never been more alluring. Standing beside her is Ares decked out in a war tunic. And Hera is presiding.

My stomach sinks into a cavernous abyss, when I realise what looms before me. I know with every fibre of my being that I must stop this ceremony. But as I ready myself to step forward, Siriarna arrives, and I stay motionless, hidden in position—watching—and waiting.

When I see Ares' sword slice through Alexandraya's

body, I desperately try to run to her. To rescue her from the chaos unfolding. But the vines shielding my hide, wrap their tendrils around my body and cover my mouth, muffling my screams, and halting my steps.

Panic rises like fire to my throat, and I wrestle with the vine to try and free myself. But it's no use, I'm left paralysed, with only a sliver of an opening serving as a window. When Alexandraya wedges the sword into the back of Ares, the thorns of dread settle in the pit of my stomach. The stems pinning me in place jiggle in a way that mimics laughter. The movement gives me enough leeway to wrestle free of their clutch, but instead of running to Alexandraya, who is now shrouded by the Furies, I bolt from the grotto, desperate to escape the tumult.

Past the peacock I race, straight to the golden chariot where I launch myself in one swift movement. Charging the reins, I direct the horses headlong toward the Main Palace. I have to get to my father, he will know what to do. Through thoughts as tangled as the vines that encapsulated me, I pray over and over to the Fates until we reach the palace.

At the grand residence I scramble in one direction after

another searching for Apollo, shouting his name relentlessly.

Psyche emerges ahead, and I meet her mystified gaze on approach. "What are you doing here?"

I don't know where to start. My words have completely escaped me, and I stand in front of the goddess tongue-tied.

She grabs my arm and I realise she's going to expel me from the palace. But, surprisingly, she drags me into a room where Zeus is standing beside an insipid looking Apollo. "Who in the realms are you?" the King of Gods bellows, the room rumbling around him.

Somehow, I manage to stand my ground and find my voice, "There is an uprising happening in a secret veiled grotto covered in vines. Hera is there. Alexandraya is there. And Ares was there." My words stop dead, just like Ares.

Apollo says to Zeus, "The destruction has begun."

"How could we have missed this? Where is Hermes? Hera?"

"She has been planning her reign for a long time," my father answers through ragged breaths. His face as pale as moonlight.

The Fates are draining the immortality from his soul with their message. I won't sit idle and watch him wither. Instinct guiding me, I reach forward and place my hands to my father's head.

When he realises what I'm doing, he feebly tries to stop me but it's too late, the connection is forged.

"Zeus, you must gather an army. All hell is about to break loose." I recite the words the Fates deliver to me in place of Apollo.

# CHAPTER 38

## Braxton

One minute I'm training with The Core on Evolirium, and the next I am ripped away by a veiled shackle to an above ground caved grotto in another realm.

A quick scan of my surroundings reveals Alexandraya, Ares, and Hera. I'm on Mount Olympus. My body tenses at the realisation, but Siriarna is nowhere in sight, and I breathe a sigh of relief. Thank the gods' for small mercies.

The Furies are positioned in front of me and the weight I have borne across my shoulders eases. My debt is about to be repaid.

Alexandraya catches my eye, and a wicked grin spreads across her face. Gnawing dread bloats my soul.

Siriarna's voice echoes through the grotto. She's trying

to stop the ceremony. It's at that precise moment that my soul wilts. I pray to the Fates that she will forgive me for not fulfilling my vow. I will not assist their rising.

I reach for her then. One last touch before I join the constellations. But a spiny hand pulls me back and a whisper reaches my ear, "You will Time freeze only Siriarna now, and allow the sacrifice to take place."

*She cannot be touched by Fury.*

A low chuckle rumbles, and the Fury continues, "Your shackle has been revoked."

*I won't do it.*

"Then your debt will pass to Paulette and we will ensure she suffers a fate worse than death," the Fury of curses hisses.

A shrieking scream releases from my lungs as I fall to my knees. Not Paulette, she has suffered enough. My guide mother does not deserve to bear the weight of my vow. My stomach churns and bile rises.

"Yes," the Fury whispers plucking the unspoken choice from my mind.

"Braxton," Siriarna yells reaching her arms forward.

"I'm sorry, Siriarna. There is no other way," I say as I bring the Ribbons of Time to my palm.

My heart shatters against my ribcage at the look in her eyes... and then I chant until the Ribbons of Time appear in my left palm. Squeezing the Sky Realm's thread between my thumb and index finger, I watch in misery as the love of my life becomes motionless. And though, I hear the commotion behind me, I only have eyes for Siriarna. Her words will always haunt me, *"I care, Braxton"*.

Pulling out the amethyst pendant I have carried with me every day since she dropped it in the meadows on Evolirium, I fasten it around her Time frozen neck. And then I stroke her cheek. Her skin beneath my touch burns more than the curse of Fury.

Red dances before my eyes, but I squeeze them shut until the blackness carries away the temptation. Along with my soul. Empty. Alone. Abandoned.

# CHAPTER 39

## Siriarna

All of a sudden, I'm alone in the grotto, and my memory is jaded. I clutch my temple to ease the migraine throbbing at its edges. And like a floodgate opening, my memories rush forth. Alexandraya, Ares, Hera. Braxton.

*Oh Braxton.*

Images of pain splayed across his face, and that sound of pure despair, replay over in my mind in slow motion. My memory stalls on the Fury whispering in his ear. The way her lips curled in a cruel smirk the moment he surrendered to his vow-traded fate. And the look of triumph radiating from Alexandraya—that's where Time stalled.

Red appears before my eyes but this time in

physicality. In front of me a river of blood steeps the earth, and a dissimilar vine clings to the rock face in front of me, this one showcasing bunches of ripe blackberries.

*What have you done, cousin?*

My hand flies to my sprinting heartbeat when I think of Braxton injured, or worse. Instead of landing on bare skin, my fingers trace a smooth cool shape and I glance down in the twilight to find my amethyst pendant sparking under the rising moonlight, hanging like a spirited reminder around my neck.

My mind is torn into what feels like a thousand directions. I need to find Braxton—I need to get to my father—I need to find my cousin.

As I ready myself to call to the Fates, Celeris dives into the grotto with stamping hooves, bucking and squealing. He lowers the wing closest to me and tilts his body sideways. His distress panics me, and I mount quickly. Through the evening air we soar, and I use my power to summon the southern winds to quicken our journey; though my stomach knots at the wonder of what has agitated my companion.

Moments later, Celeris lands in the hollow. He throws my body from his back, and I hit the ground with a thud.

What I am confronted with is a sight so distressing that my breath catches in my throat and my heart thrashes with such force, it bruises my ribcage.

Before me, the Crocus flowers have wilted, all but one are shrivelled, brown, and lifeless. Jagged cracks in the earth are all that remains of the pool Celeris created centuries ago. The moisture completely evaporated.

A tremble from the once vibrant yellow throat of the last remaining flower begins to still. I can't bear to watch him die. With shaking hands, I dig my fingers into the ground, careful not to break the roots, and pluck the flower from the parched earth.

Crocus goes limp in my hand.

Celeris squeals in a high pitched tone.

And I weep.

I bring the flower close to my lips so I can whisper to its dying soul. "I'm sorry I could not rescue you. Nor save you from the curse you did not deserve," I say utterly wretched.

My breath expels in a plume of visible air not unlike the curlicue on my arms that has started to tingle. It swirls from my lips to flower in a slow, purposeful gust, winding its way down the pale yellow throat of Crocus.

The flower begins to tremble in my hand, and I cling to its form, desperate to hold onto the mortal cursed flower. But the vibration becomes so violent that I can no longer hold onto it, and it plummets to the ground.

I can't bear to watch. I can't bear to see the last of Crocus, so I turn my back and close my eyes, even though the last of daylight is sinking away, and shadows already obscure my vision.

"Siriarna," the ethereal voices of the Fates chime behind me.

My shoulders slump as I realise I have failed in my divine destiny.

"Siriarna," the voices repeat.

As slow as the setting sun, I turn to face my new fate. And when I do, I am confronted with a sight that stings my eyes with unexpected joy. Crocus, in mortal form, standing beside Celeris, The Fates, hovering in translucent spirit form behind them.

# CHAPTER 40

## Alexandraya

Arriving at the peak of the Sky Realm, I drop my prey and circle the palace—free as a bird.

Braxton smacks the ground hard, his body limp, but breathing. And he doesn't try to rise.

My feet soon after thud to the ground as I morph from visceral to figure at will. It's time to make my reluctant ally comfortable in his new home.

Long strides bring me to his person, and I use my foot to flip him onto his back. His eyes burn with hatred in the faded daylight, but he does not speak. The silence is a mercy. With one hand, I grab the neck of his shirt and pull him to the crook of my arm. His weight is hefty in his slumped form, but with new strength and vigour, the task is effortless.

Into the palace I march; past the fresco room, and office, and into the kitchen. With my elbow I slide the door under the archway open, and flick on the rickety light that glows dim from the depths below. Then I tread down the spiral staircase humming Melodie's song of victory. When I reach the dank ground of the pits of the palace, I unload Braxton into the dungeon's cell and secure the manacles around his wrists. "Sorry for the shackles Braxton, but I must make sure you can't reverse time," I say.

"Do what you will," he answers in a flat tone.

It's his face that betrays his true emotions, a look of self-loathing and shame. I doubt he'd reverse time even if given the chance. He has betrayed Siriarna. He has abandoned his soul.

Which makes me think of Hermes. Was sacrificing a chance at true love worth the reward of immortality?

*Yes.*

I am what I was always meant to be.

Love is a myth. Power is the true gift.

And I have never felt more present.

The trial of absolution.

# ACKNOWLEDGMENTS

Thank you to all the people who have taken a chance on reading this novel. Without your support of my journey into authorhood, this novel wouldn't have seen the light of day. I am truly grateful.

I am one of the lucky ones, whose family have been my solid rocks, my A team, my cheerleaders. So many days and nights have I bombarded my mum, Judy Eckford, and sister, Abigail Jane with cries for help. Thank you for keeping me on track and helping through patches of writer's block.

My husband, daughter and son are my true inspiration. They have witnessed me lock myself in my room and write for hours upon hours, and never complained. Thank you for your encouragement, edits, reading and rereading and reading again; and for helping me bring this novel to life.

## Contact Prudence Willett

Instagram | TikTok | Facebook : @prudencewillettwrites

Website: prudencewillett.com

## Leave a Review

If you loved Alexandraya, please consider leaving a positive review. Word of mouth is also a great way to introduce your friends to the Divine Destinies Trilogy.

The trilogy concludes with Book 3, available soon.